UNLEASH THE BEAST

Werewolf Shifter Romance

A. H. Leigh

Copyright © 2021 A. H. Leigh

All rights reserved

The characters and events portrayed in this book are fictitious. Any similarity to real persons, living or dead, is coincidental and not intended by the author.

No part of this book may be reproduced, or stored in a retrieval system, or transmitted in any form or by any means, electronic, mechanical, photocopying, recording, or otherwise, without express written permission of the publisher.

ISBN-13: 9798589603439

ISBN-10: B08R867ZYP

Cover design by: Art Painter
Library of Congress Control Number: 2018675309
Printed in the United States of America

CONTENTS

Title Page
Copyright
Introduction
Chapter 1   1
Chapter 2   11
Chapter 3   16
Chapter 4   24
Chapter 5   30
Chapter 6   38
Chapter 7   50
Chapter 8   53
Chapter 9   64
Chapter 10   77
Chapter 11   89
Chapter 12   101
Chapter 13   106
Chapter 14   111
Chapter 15   119
Chapter 16   123
Chapter 17   130
Chapter 18   139

| About The Author | 149 |
| Books By This Author | 151 |

INTRODUCTION

Isabella being a first year in college and the youngest of three children, is the only of her siblings whom stills lives at home with her parents. When they move to the outskirts of town so her father can easily conduct research for work in their front yard, strange shadows start appearing in the woods. One being more constant than the rest.

CHAPTER 1

Isabella awoke to the sound of her mother's screams.

"Henry! Did you do this?" her mother, Teresa, yelled.

Isabella decided to check out what was happening despite the lack of sunlight. The girl still had a bit of trouble navigating her way through the new house. She let out a cry when her foot hit a moving box near the arch leading into the kitchen from the hall. Her mother was at the doorway on the other side of the room looking at something on the back porch.

"What is it?" her father, Henry, said as he walked past the girl and towards his wife.

"I like to think of myself as a supportive and open minded woman. I don't mind living out in the middle of nowhere so you can do you science in peace. But damn it Henry, keep the dead vermin off my porch." her mother finished.

The past few days the family had awoken to a few small dead animals resting on their doorstep. Isabella tried to catch a glimpse of today's creature. No matter how much she stretched her height, she couldn't see over her father. The man crouched down to pick up the animal and that's when Isabella saw the lifeless rabbit. The poor animals never looked like they died of natural cause either. They always glimmered with blood matted in their fur and open wounds littered their carcass. It wasn't hard to figure out they were fresh kills and left like some kind of sick joke. Isabella hating seeing the dead animal, but this one made her realize something. She snapped out of her daze upon her father's return with a bundle of paper towels.

"Wait, dad wait, don't move it yet, I want to see something." Isabella said as she turned and headed for her room. Dodging the out of place boxes on her way, she retrieved her in a matter of seconds. On her way back to the crime scene, she was too focused on the photo app and caught her pinky toe on a rug. She hopped on one foot as she scrolled through her pictures from yesterday.

It had been a warm day in mid-May and Isabella was taking advantage of it. A perk of living in a forest was a massive lack of neighbors. This was a benefit on days like today where the girl could plug in her phone and blare Super Junior while doing homework. She sat on the grass in her backyard a.k.a the small bit of flat land behind her house that grew into a denser site of trees. Sitting with folded legs, she laid her work on her lap and glanced at the shaking foliage ahead. Curious, but not brave enough to move, she froze until whatever rustled the leaves left. Feeling around the plush grass for her pen, she saw something out of the corner of her eye. Turning her head, Isabella saw an orange and cream colored bunny rabbit a few feet beside her.

"It's so cute," she said aloud to herself. Making no sudden movements, the obsidian haired girl grabbed the speakers and lifted her phone. She couldn't turn the music off, the rabbit could notice and get scared. Not taking her eyes off the ball of fluff for one second, Isabella opened her camera app and angled for a perfect shot. She clicked the button and a shutter sound echoed over the loud pop music. The bunny turned its head and hopped away. The girl let out a sigh while checking the image she managed to capture. Regardless of the blur from the rabbit whipping its head around, it was adorable.

Now Isabella felt a frown grow on her face as she matched yesterday's image to today's victim. The lifeless fuzz was, in fact, the cute bunny from yesterday.

"I feel like I'm a target," Isabella said. Her parents took turns glancing at the image trying to understand.

"Would you, um, like to bury it?" her father asked, trying to provide comfort.

"No, I want to find out who is doing this."

Jeremy remembers when he first heard the news, he didn't think it was true. not because it seemed outrageous, he knew things like this happened sometimes. It was because he heard it come from a lady who rumored to use a crystal ball to predict fortunes.

It had been almost a decade ago. Jeremy and his friends were at the age of being able to go a few places on their own. That night was a time of rituals and sacrifices. It was a carnival of fenced areas to condition teenagers and tents of elders conducting dark magic. The small village came together like this every full moon. At the awkward age of twelve, the boy and his group started to show up but were still too young to take part. Of the few options they had, the purple hut with gold trim with the foreign fortune teller seemed most amusing.

Jeremy grew up not using too many words. His

people communicated more with visual cues and body language rather than verbal expressions. He watched enough television to be able to understand spoken language, but never had the opportunity to use it. As the group of coal haired boys went inside, Jeremy couldn't help his mild excitement from the chance to talk like a real human. Even if it was getting told some random string of events that would take place in his future by some strange lady. The seven of them bowed in the entrance, front of the table the fortune teller was sat behind. In the midst of them saying muddled greetings, the lady spoke up.

"You boys, oh you young things, don't strain yourselves. I know what you are and I know of the distraught in front of you. Come here, come sit down."

Since the ratio of boys to chairs was not equal, they looked to one another. Jason, who liked acting like the one in charge, took the seat on the left. As Jackson was about to make a move for the other stool, the woman caught their attention.

"You," she said with her eyes resting on Jeremy.

"Me?" he questioned, trying to be casual when his voice cracked on the first letter.

"Sit," she said as she nodded to the empty seat.

During this, the boys stopped their shuffling and stared at the one she called out. Either this woman was a good actress or had real news to tell them. Jeremy took his seat but didn't allow himself to relax in the cushion.

"Yes?" he questioned with his eyes having never left the stranger's face.

"I know what you boys are." she said, shaking her pointer finger in their direction. "You," she said, pointing at Jeremy. "All you," she said looking each of the boys in the eyes. She noticed how young they must have been by the lack of color in their irises. "This whole village," she said with a flare of her nostrils. "All you are those werethings," she said.

Jeremy could feel Jackson rolling his eyes from behind him. He agreed that she was being dramatic. They all assumed the woman must have caught on since they had seen her at the other full moon events.

"I will never understand how they've managed to be so quiet for so long. Regardless, you little wolf boys, you must know of humans, yes?" she stated more than asked. A few of them let out muffled agreements and Jackson went so far to say "of course".

"So you boys know of how many centuries your kind has longed to be with them, to feel like they belong? Hmm?" she said. The boys nodded this time. Jeremy knew the feeling well. He felt it every time their people went into a panic over any potential sighting of a human. He felt it when his family journeyed to a city and grew jealous of how open they communicated. He felt it when he saw commercials for fast food, knowing he could never try it due to the food's chemicals his body couldn't handle. He felt it when he got strange looks from others in the village if he sang along to whatever music was playing his his earbuds. He knew the feeling and he felt it often. He hadn't learned much of the non-romantic relationship between humans and werewolves. What he believes to be true is the humans in power know of werewolf's existence. The humans choose to leave werewolves be, with the intent of avoiding conflict.

"Well, have you boys learned the differences in human mating and werewolf mating?" the woman asked. Disgruntled noises and a few snickers came from the pre-teens.

"No." Jackson said as he stifled a laugh, remembering the talk his parents gave him a few weeks ago.

"We know things. " Jason struggled to communicate. Despite his self-proclaimed title as the leader, he didn't know much spoken language. Jeremy took this chance to converse with the foreigner.

"Werewolves have a set mate, the only one they can love and ever reproduce with. It's decided by the moon and there is a small," he paused to give his voice a break, not ever having spoken so much at once. "sliver of a chance it could be a human. That's how werewolves came to be, the moon made a wolf's mate to be a human as punishment." he finished, catching his breath. He felt a few hands patting his back and heard a couple sounds of congratulations.

"What a smart boy. So, do you know about human mating?" she asked and the boys broke out in laughter. Jeremy took the question serious and wanted to respond.

"Yes. They can love whoever they want." the boy replied.

"They almost never love ours." Mark said from his spot to the right of Jeremy. It seems like the boy had been practicing but not yet perfected his grammar. Jeremy gave him a look meaning well done since he at least tried.

"The werewolves? Yes boy, your right. But look at you all, there has been enough success to have gotten your kind this far." she said with a tone of excitement. It was true, human and werewolves sometimes reproduced. It helped the race become more of the fairer species with each successful pairing. This led for Jeremy's generation to have about ninety four percent human dna. This was just enough to be human until adolescence. On a werewolf's thirteenth birthday, they become cursed to be a wolf on the full moon.

"But yes, from what I've learned, it's rare. Of the one percent of werewolf and human pairings, a fraction are successful." the woman said. Jeremy had pieced together where this conversation was going.

"Yes, you, smart boy," she said looking at Jeremy. So maybe this woman was a mind reader? Or just had perfect timing for what she was going to say.

"Yes, that is what I need to tell you boys. I have seen it since your group stepped into my workspace. It hit me so strong that I didn't even need my sphere to clarify it." she said while gesturing to the crystal ball sitting off to the side behind her desk. "One of you boys is essential to your generation of werethings." she paused her roaming gaze on Jeremy for what felt like the thousandth time. She watched the boy gulp his anxiety as he was guessing what she was about to say.

"You, You are Park Jeremy, correct?" she asked, pointing at the boy seated in front of her.

"Yes," he said with a nod. The woman let out a sigh of content. She liked the village's people and often prayed for their well being. She was ecstatic that a smart boy like him would be the moon's choice this time around.

"You, Park Jeremy, will have a human mate."

CHAPTER 2

Isabella was unsure of the best course of action. She felt a bit attached to the dead thing and couldn't toss it in the trash. It may also contain things that would help in tracking what was doing this. The girl lay awake in bed, unable to fall back asleep due to these thoughts. Once the sun had risen, the girl came the conclusion that police would be useless. Considering she herself was unsure of the event, the officials might not even care.

She wanted to just forget about it, mark it off as random and hope it stops happening. But, the more she thought about it, the less random it seemed. Isabella remembered the day before the first incident. On her walk home from school, she admired two birds play fighting near her house. The next morning, victim number one was a small sparrow. Day two had been an identical bird. Day three was a squirrel she had managed to get near before it scampered away the evening. Isabella loved all the woodland creatures neighboring her new home. Back in the city, she seldom saw a single bird fly past her apartment complex. She wanted to enjoy the cute things, not have them killed. The girl got out of bed and walked to the kitchen and grabbed a bottle of water from the fridge.

Isabella approached the back door and opened it, greeted with an empty concrete slab. With a small frown, she assumed her father threw the thing away. The microwave's display read 9:23. With having no other plans for this Sunday, Isabella decided to do a bit of investigating. The girl ran and slipped on a pair of shoes before leaving the house. She left through the back door and strolled around the yard. She opened the bottle and took a drink, stopping in her work spot from the preceding day. Her eyes landed on the bush that caught her attention before the rabbit incident. Was it rustling like that before she left the house?

For a split second, the wild idea of a monster came to mind but soon dismissed. She grew up with a scientist as a father. She knew better than to get worried over the unknown or believe in fairy tales. Any thoughts she had as a child of mystical beings were always refuted by her parents. Her mother would start with a "don't believe in that nonsense". The woman's statements would be confirmed by Isabella's father with bits of fact.

"Daddy, there is a monster in my closet," the six-year-old Isabella would tell her father.

"Sweetie, monsters aren't real," he would reply.

"Says who?" she asks.

"Says your father the ecologist that has inspected your closet several times. The only proof of life he has ever found are the half eaten pieces of broccoli you hide in the back," he says.

These exchanges would be enough to make the young girl confident in her safety. They also made her embarrassed enough to not ask many questions.

"Dad, the moon is cheese," the girl told her father. The man rolled his eyes.

"What idiot told you that?" he asked.

"A lot of the kids at school say that," she said.

"No sweetheart, the moon is made up of dirt. The moon came to be billions of years ago when a large object hit Earth and blasted out rocks. These rocks came together and orbited our planet. They melted together, cooled down and became the Moon," he stated.

"Then how are there big holes in the moon if it's not made of cheese with the holes in it?" she asked, feeling as if she found a flaw in her father's statement.

The man wanted to play along and let the little girl believe in her own ideas. But to have his daughter be intelligent seemed more rewarding. So, he always made sure to set her straight.

"For another 500 million years pieces of rock kept hitting the Moon. That's why there are craters. Those big dents are craters, not holes. Holes go all the way through while craters are just dips in the surface. Like the dimples on your face." He said while tickling his daughters cheek to made her smile. The girl laughed, showing off her cheek craters.

Having all her nineteen years filled with facts didn't

leave much room for fantasy. When Isabella saw the bushes tremble, she wrote it off as other creatures playing. Even as the rumble followed her as she walked around the property, she didn't think much of it.

CHAPTER 3

Jeremy was not a fan of his hormones. This was something that came with adolescence and lingered into adulthood. Also, his senses became enhanced around the time of the full moon ever since his shift. As the boy grew older, he understood more and more why having a human mate was so glorified. Having to become wolf was the worst thing he has ever experienced. Even at age twenty-two, he remembers his first transformation in vivid detail.

September 22nd, his own birthday eight years ago had been a day full of angst and fear for the boy. A few of his friends had already started shifting so it wasn't all foreign. Mother nature disregarded the Korean way of counting age. It had their kind begin the lifelong horror of shapeshifting at international age thirteen. They all became well educated about the process. The boys had been counting down the days for Mark to undergo the experience. All nervous, the year before anyone else in their group would have to do it.

"Are you excited?" Jackson teased Mark as they all sat in the latter's front yard.

"You better be ready, because when I grow claws, you'll be the first I go after." Mark said, throwing his arm round Jackson's neck and putting him in a headlock.

"Everyone says it hurts, are you scared?" Tyler asked, worried for his friend yet relieved he had years until it was his turn. Mark just shrugged.

"I mean, there's nothing I can do. I just have to let it happen and toughen it out." he said, having released Jackson and leaned back.

"It happens at midnight, right?" Brandon asked.

"Duh. Why does it have to be on our birthdays though? Why can't it wait until the first full moon of the year or something? That way Jackson, Jer and I can all get it over at once." Jason said, wondering why it would have to be so spaced out.

"You just don't want all the attention to be on you when it happens. You'll be so scared that you'll piss yourself." Jeremy said, teasing his friend. Jason looked at him and nodded with a scowl, inviting the boy to fight him. The other boys just laughed.

The sun fell faster as the young boys sat around. They did their best to distract each other from the upcoming event. The moon was high in the sky before any of them dared to bring it up.

"What time is now?" Steve asked. Jason pulled out his flip phone and check the time.

"11:47." he asked. The boy looked over at Mark who seemed tenser as the seconds ticked by. "How do you feel?" he asked.

Mark just nodded and gave a weak smile. "Okay I guess." he said while his inner voice was screaming at him that he was anything but.

Seeing his friend under so much pressure, Jackson decided to lift the mood. He threw his head back towards the sky and started howling. "Ahhhooouuuuuu, aaaahhhhhoooouuu" the boy let out between laughs. He paused to look at his friends before continuing. A few of the other boys soon joined in. After a few rounds of this they all were looking at the sky and giggling between fake howls. Excluding the one who would be a real wolf before the night was over, of course.

"You guys all suck." Mark said as he laughed. The boys kept up the act for a bit longer. They became caught up enough to not notice Mark's first few twitches. After a large convulsion, Jason stopped, causing the other boys to follow suit.

"Oh shit." Jackson said as he watched Mark let out ragged breaths.

Jason checked the clock for the second time that night. "Guys, it's midnight." He said with worry in his tone.

"No duh." Tyler said, but no one heard it as Mark let

out a cry that made them wince in pain.

    A surprise to everyone, Jeremy was the first to react as he got up to rush to his friend's side. "Mark, Mark, I'm taking off your clothes okay. Don't think I weird, but remember they told us to do this, okay? They told us to do this so it wouldn't get caught in your skin as you shift, okay? This way we all won't have to see your bare ass for too long once you come back." Jeremy said in a calm voice as he removed his friend's shirt.

    Mark didn't respond, but no one expected him too. It was clear to the boys during the many lessons that the first shift was a shock to the body. Their friend would become even less responsive as he became more canine. It was advised to have people who would help you near during your first time. It was lucky that the group was close in age and trusted each other. None of them would hesitate to help each other.

    Jason and the others went to Mark and got him undressed as his skin was overtaken by fur. Bones snapped and cracked as the boy fell to the ground. A few of his friends shifted to help him but thought better and let nature take its course. Some neighbors had their lights on by now, but no one exited their home. The small community kept track of everything dealing with shifting. It was well known that the boy would going through his first transformation tonight. It wasn't so much dangerous as it was awkward to be around someone during their first time. The village had respect for one another. People observed from behind closed doors for a moment then let the boys be.

Mark had always been the quiet one of the group, and this rang true even now. Outside of his initial cry at midnight, he didn't make too much noise. His friends stood in awe at the beast before them. Jason grabbed his flip phone once again.

"12:25, It took him less than an hour. Psh, show off." Jason said, bringing up the mood.

Wolves were different than humans, though obvious, it was sometimes forgotten. When Jackson tried to step towards Mark, he became surprised at his friend's growls. The boys all held their breath and took a step back. Temperament was the most frightening part of the transformation. What happened during the time as canine was almost never recalled the morning after. This had a good amount of disadvantage at the beginning of the people's history. After years of this they learned more about what to do to avoid tragedy.

"Guys, let's give him some space. If he doesn't head for the woods soon, we should just stay calm and let him do what he wants. We're his friends, his human instincts should be strong enough to let him not hurt us." Jeremy said, recalling some things they learned from their elders. The boys let out noises of agreement and without thinking sat back down.

Mark didn't like the sudden movement. This, shown by his barks and snarls after Steve, the last to sit, crossed his legs. The wolf lowered his head and sniffed around him. The boys looked at one another with wide eyes.

"Breathe, it's okay." Jackson said, sounding more like he was comforting himself than the people around him. Brandon began breathing in through his nose and out his mouth. Steve closed his eyes and pretended to be on Jeju island.

"I think after Mark shifts back, he's going to be confused when he looks in a mirror." Tyler said as the wolf broke his stare with the boy and moved on sniffing the grass again. This statement was true since the coal haired boy shifted into a wolf with dark red fur. As known by their people, whatever color fur you have as a wolf will be the color of any hair on your body. It was rare for a werewolf to have fur any color than black, dark red or brown wasn't too odd. It did mean something significant. There hasn't been a red or brown wolf in a couple hundred years, the boy didn't know what it meant. With no lesson on specific fur color that they could recall, so if must not be too important.

"I wonder if I dyed my hair pink before I shifted, what color my fur would be." Brandon wondered aloud.

"Your fur would be black, or maybe red like Mark or something. But not pink, I don't think the moon cares about having wolves with pink fur." Tyler said, not knowing the answer but pretended that he did.

Mark seemed to have had enough with their small chat. He raised his head with perked ears and dashed into the mass of trees beside his house. As the sound of the wolves paws were no longer heard, several of the boys let out dramatic sighs. A few of them even letting themselves fall back onto the grass in relief.

"We're going to have to do this six more times." Steve said with a whine.

CHAPTER 4

Still unresolved on what to do, Isabella glanced at the old shed. It was a part of the property that was there when they moved in. The small room was under construction by her father to become his own workspace. The man was in the space, so Isabella decided to ask his opinion.

"Hello." Isabella said as she spotted him in the shed. He lifted his head from his sketches. The papers sat on a modern table that looked out of place in the worn out room.

"May I help you?" he said as he shifted in his seat, which matched the table but not the concrete floor.

"Well, maybe." she said as she walked further into the room. She turned around in a full circle letting her eyes wander over the cracking walls. Her eyes landed on the single window that was above her father's workspace. "What is the most probable cause of the dead animals on our doorstep?" she asked, trying to sound serious about the matter, hoping for a serious answer.

The man stretched his legs and let out a groan. He wasn't a big man, but by Korea's standards, he was a little heavier than average. He scratched his head full of hair poking up at odd angles, not having brushed it since he woke up. "I'd say it's just a random wild dog. This house has been empty for a while, so it may be happy to have a neighbor." he said, tone not confident and trying his best to not sound like he was making it up on the spot.

"So, it's like, leaving them as gifts?" she said, starting to believe his theory. Still weary on why the animals she interacted with having to become the victims. That part didn't seem too necessary in giving gifts of random dead animals.

"Sure, but I would think that they would be more territorial. It is odd at how friendly it or they are being." he said. Her father's entire job was to observe how animals interact with their environment. Any opinions he had were more so fact than a guess. The cog wheel of Isabella's mind started churning. The reason they moved out here was for her father to work from home. Now odd animal stuff was happening.

"Is that what why you wanted to come out here? Did you already know about this and wanted to research it or whatever?" she asked, thinking she cracked the non-existent code.

"No, I just enjoy the foliage." he said. The girl rolled her eyes.

"So you do know something. What is it?" she asked, hoping he wasn't just trying to get her to leave him alone by ignoring her. The man turned back in his chair and now faced the window.

"I didn't believe them, so they insisted I check on it myself." he said as he went back to sketching his ideal interior. The room stayed silent as she waited for more information that never came. She tilted her head as she watched her father ignore her and carry on with his work. It was typical for the man to be open with his answers to the few questions Isabella ever asked. So this kind of response was strange. A bit confused by what he said, or more so the lack thereof, she left the shed. The girl walked around the yard and felt her pockets for her phone, which was not on her. She remembered getting up after the sunrise and leaving the device under her pillow. Not wanting to go all the way back inside, she continued her wandering.

Maybe she should just conduct her own research. She was in college and majoring in biological sciences. Still unsure of what particular title she would want once she graduated. Research was her favorite nerdy thing to do, the only part of school she enjoyed. The girl looked over at the forever rustling bushes. It could be the thing her father didn't want to tell her about. That seemed like the most important place to look but also the most dangerous. The girl decided grabbing her phone would be worth it, just in case. She didn't want to become one of those dumb girls you see in those low budget horror movies.

She tossed the now empty water bottle in the recycling after grabbing her phone. She needed a game plan. She could just walk into the forest and look around a bit. It didn't seem too dangerous since they've been living near it for four days. The worst that's happened it dead animal presents. Isabella took a deep breath as she pulled back the branches of the now stagnant bush. The tall plants seemed placed by decades ago, due to them now being taller than the girl. to serve as a barrier between the flatland and where the trees started to grow. She stepped into the leaves and saw trunks of the hanging trees. Nothing had popped out and said 'boo' yet so she was still in the clear.

Isabella let out her breath and unlocked her phone. It was 11:34 and she had a few texts from school friends about assignments. She ignored them and opened the camera. All she saw ahead were trees far enough apart to see more trees maybe fifteen feet ahead. There was plenty of space to weave through. She checked the ground and noticed that where she stood was free of grass. It led to a dirt trail that turned more grassy the further it went into the woods. It seemed that someone, or thing, came through this passage enough to leave a path. But, it stopped behind the bush? The girl turned around and lifted the limbs of the bush to see the ground full of grass and clovers.

In less than a minute she made this not so fun discovery. Something comes from the forest and stops in front of the bush rather often. Maybe left over from before she moved in? Dirt trails lasted for a long time, so it seemed plausible. Still a bit creepy, to think that something from the wild came and lurked behind the bush. Isabella face palmed herself. That's why the bushed always moved, not because of harmless animals shaking the branches. But because a strange thing came and hid there. The girl tensed and wanted to turn back. She took deep breaths and closed her eyes, if she left now she knew she would be too scared to come again. She had to do this now and get it over with.

As she opened her eyes, she saw her phone with the camera still open. The girl stepped backwards and aimed the device at the ground. About to take a picture of where the dirt path leads to the spot, she heard leaves rustle. This made her jump and she hit the button mid spaz, releasing the loud shutter sound.

"Oh my god, calm down." she said to herself with her hand over her heart, feeling the organ pump fast from the scare. She disregarded the first image, knowing it would be blurry. Isabella repositioned herself to take a more crisp picture. Satisfied the second time around, the locked her phone and turned around. She regretted it as she saw someone standing in front of her.

"Hi." he said.

CHAPTER 5

Jeremy could recall all his friends first transformations. They fell into a routine and learned the best course of action. They all gained experience each time around and were happy to have no complications. What Jeremy remembered from his first time was the fumble of clothes, and pain. Bones cracking and fuzz spreading everywhere, even to places he didn't know he had. He remembered feeling like death, then waking up naked by a river he never saw before. Out of all seven boys, they said Jeremy had run the furthest. It took most of the night and morning to track him down and many adults heckled him. They said he was trying to find his rumored human mate.

The boys wouldn't learn any details of their mate. That was something that happened according to the moon and no one could predict. The boys did end up spreading the news of a fortune teller saying Jeremy had a human mate. It fit the people's lineage. Several of them teased him about it every now and then. There were a few things that could be foreseen or figured out. Though it was with spells and potions and odd things the mystical of their people did. Few took those tellings serious due to them almost never being accurate.

The one thing that was questionable was Mark's fur color. As proven by Brandon during his first transition, the moon did not care about chemicals that changed hair color when it came to wolf fur. The younger boy dyed a patch of hair bright pink to test his theory. When the boy shifted, he had jet black fur, the same as most of the other boys in the group. The one outlier was the kid with now dark red human hair and wolf fur to match.

The teachers of the village knew that different color fur meant different things. According to documents from the past, dark red fur meant misfortune, madness. The first, and last, person on record to have red fur was almost five hundred years ago. The man in question started off his life as a sweet kid, rather quiet and kind towards others. He went through his first few transitions awkward and wild. This nothing but normal for a thirteen-year-old wolf boy. Then came his sixteenth birthday. This was often when werewolves would start feeling a pull towards their mate, the closer the mate, the stronger the pull. It was alright if the pull didn't happen until eighteen, or even twenty. But the minimal age had always been sixteen.

When the red-furred teen started to feel odd, he guessed the pull was starting. He told his friends and parents and they were happy for him. Most of them even offered advice and support. They wished him good fortune with whoever she was and told him to let her come to him. Don't worry when they would be together. He took this advice and carried on with his life as your average wolf boy for a few months.

Mid-November, six months past his sixteenth birthday, is when he saw her. He thought she was the most perfect being, more so than he could have imagined. Despite her being a human claimed by an estranged acquaintance, he felt the pull. Once he laid eyes on her, his mind went wild and his breathing became erratic. She was across the way, holding hands with that other guy. A few seconds passed and she glanced in his direction. She saw the odd boy, wide-eyed and huffing his chest, and became nervous.

"Who is he?" she asked, tugging on her boyfriend's hand to get his attention. The boy looked at her, following her line of vision to the red-haired boy in the distance.

"Baekhyun, are you alright?" the boy asked, yelling over the noise of the crowd in front of them. The couple was at the full moon festival, with all the other young adults who would shift.

The overwhelmed boy took a few slow breaths and walked towards them. "Yeah, Chanyeol, I'm fine." he said with a forced smile. He stopped a few feet in front of them and clenched his fist. His senses, her scent, the hormones raging through him. The other guy she liked, she liked him more. She didn't know Baekhyun yet, but she was his, she was his so why was she with Chanyeol? "Who is this?" he asked, blinking as he gulped, was he transitioning right now? Why did his insides feel so shattered?

"This is Jieun, my mate," Chanyeol said with a bright smile as he looked at the girl. Upon seeing her cocked eyebrow, he remembered to correct himself. "Girlfriend, she's my girlfriend," he finished, relieved as the girl nodded.

"Okay" was all Baekhyun said. He forced himself away from the crowd, away from the couple, the girl. The girl who was with another guy who claimed her as his mate. Baekhyun felt so stupid. Why was he feeling this way towards a girl who would never be his? Did the world hate him, did the moon not care about his feelings? This was a sick joke to the boy. For the past half of a year, he loved the foreign feelings. They told him he would find her, the one, the one person he could love forever and spend his life with. As a young hopeless romantic, he looked forward to meeting his mate for years now. When it became known that he had the pull so young, he felt like it was the start of a fairytale.

Now he knew why he had the strange red fur, becoming the odd one out in any and everything he did. Becoming the tail end of sly jokes from his friends. It was because the universe thought he was a joke, a damn fool. The boy sat by a boulder near the festival. He wasn't suppose to leave the area. He needed to stay and 'interact' or whatever the elders said. At this low point, he saw it as another way the world was teasing him. Forcing him to stay near all the happy young couples, he felt the urge to rip their throats out. All he wanted to do right now was throw himself into the nearby river. Hoping no one cared enough to question his disappearance.

The moon was nearing its peak as the people started to leave the small grounds and spread out. Baekhyun stood up from his spot, wiping at the stray tears collected at the bottom of his jaw. He looked at the crowd just in time to catch sight of the girl he thought would be his, kiss that other guy. The fragile boy turned his head, wanting to vomit at the puppy love between the couple. He started to feel the crack of his bones, or maybe it was his heart. He ran over to the fence and climbed it, wanting to get away as fast as possible.

The boy never shifted back. During the night, he attacked the girl. This prompted a battle between him and her boyfriend while in their wolf forms. The red wolf being much smaller and younger didn't stand a chance. The black wolf slaughtered Baekhyun. Chanyeol was overridden with guilt once he awoke and learned what he had done. Soon the girl recovered from her moderate injuries the red wolf inflicted. She and the coal haired man lived their lives together. They had a total of three happy children and several grandkids.

"I hope you don't end up like that." Brandon whispered to Mark after the lecture was over. The boy got smacked on the back of the head by Jeremy.

"He won't end up like that. He has us, he knows he can tell us anything." Jeremy said, directing the last part at Mark.

"It's okay, I don't even want a mate anyway." Mark said shrugging his shoulders.

"You're so full of it. You are the sappiest person I have ever met. I'd feel bad for whatever girl gets stuck with you. Not because you'd try to kill her. But because you would smother her with all the mushy shit you come up with." Jackson said.

The years passed, and Mark had never expressed feeling the pull. Now in their early twenties, Mark and Jeremy were the last of the group to not have felt it. Even Tyler, the youngest of the group, had a girl he's interested in.

"It's because you all got lucky and had it happen early. It's not like we're old and gray and never laid." Jeremy said, a bit upset at another one of his friend's remarks.

"Woah, okay, chill out Jer. I'm sure you'll find the human girl soon enough." Jason said, a bit playful but also somewhat serious.

"Yeah, and whoever is for Mark must have heard he was a red head and ran for the hills," Jackson added with a mocking grin.

"It's not like you've met your mate yet though." Mark said as he took a sip from Jackson's glass of water. They were over the latter's house, inside despite it being a sunny day in late april.

"Whatever man, at least I've started to feel stuff, unlike you two emotionless old men," Jackson said, grabbing the glass back and chugging the remnants.

"You're six months older than me." Jeremy said with narrowed eyes and head tilted.

Jackson set his glass on the table in front of him and leaned back into the couch. He threw his feet onto the wooden surface and crossed one leg over the other. "We're all men here." he said.

This made Steve laugh. "Is that why you like to cuddle whenever someone spends the night?" he said from his spot between the armrest and the boy he was teasing. That prompted Jackson to lean towards him and lay his head on his shoulder.

"Yes" he said as he wrapped his arms around Steve's waist. Steve just let out a mock annoyed scoff and let one of the other boys change the subject.

CHAPTER 6

Her heartbeat rose and she heard pounding in her ears. Any moisture in her mouth disappear. She didn't freeze like how the people always seemed to in movies. Instead, she stared at the boy and took a step back before stopping. This was her house, kind of. What right did he have to be here? She thought of something to say, but he spoke up again.

"Are you okay?" he asked, his voice sounding a bit shaky. Was he nervous too? Why was he asking if she was okay, she came from her house, he came from nowhere. Before she could catch herself, she spoke.

"Are *you* okay?" she asked, with her face scrunched in confusion and mild annoyance. He tilted his head a bit and looked at her. Maybe he lives around here too, there wouldn't be a random guy in the woods.

"I think so," he said before cracking a small smile. He was kind of attractive. No, scratch that, he was straight up adorable. But this just made her more on edge.

"I live" she started before pointing behind her "there. We just moved in," she said. He nodded at her and look to where she was pointing.

"You live in a bush?" he asked, trying not to laugh.

Her face dropped, he must think she's so weird. "No, like, there's a house and I live" she paused to let out a shaky breath "in it," she said as she gulped. He kept looking at her, eyes roaming all over her face and body. She didn't feel uncomfortable, but just like she should make a good first impression. Deep down, she wanted to be able to see this guy again. She was trying to be friendly that way he might not try to avoid her forever. They stared at each other for a moment. She soon realized she should finish her story.

"And I live there, with my parents, not by myself, that'd be weird." she said, eyes still locked on his. He didn't say anything so she felt the need to keep talking. "We moved in four days ago, maybe five, I can't remember. But the thing is, um." she paused, not sure if she should tell him about the animals and if that would weird him out. He raised his eyebrows, questioning her why she stopped mid-sentence. She decided it wasn't important and to just skip over it. "I just wanted to look and see what's back here. I was nervous, that's why I kinda freaked out. I thought I was going to die, maybe, but you're not dead so I guess it's safe." she finished, feeling stupid at her awkward explanation.

"I'm not dead." he said with a chuckle.

"Nope, you're alive," she said. He made no move to reply and kept his eyes on hers. She stood there for a second, then blinked a few times before checking her phone. She didn't remember the time it read once she put it in the back pocket of her jeans.

"I should uh, um," she said, taking a step forward, but he didn't move. She went to walk around him, but his voice made her freeze.

"Would you like a tour?" he asked from her right.

She looked up at him, he being a head taller. She had no idea what he meant by tour and the rough look in his eyes made her want to run away. During his internal battle, he smiled and grabbed her wrist.

"Let's go." he said.

For whatever reason, she didn't mind going through the woods with the strange boy. He could be taking her to a witch's house and turned into stew and she wouldn't mind. They started the walk by going forward until the dirt path disappeared. Then he turned her to the right and they went closer to a thin body of water.

"I didn't know there was a creek back here." she said.

The boy looked at her and slid his hand down into hers. The girl checked their hands while the boy brought himself closer to the ground. He tugged on her hand to sit next to him. Isabella sat on the forest floor and looked at the water in front of her. This was nice, random, but nice. The only other experience she had with guys was one or two 'boyfriends'. She only hung around them during high school. Even those lasted for just a few weeks before they would get bored with each other. Even though she just met this boy, sitting by the water and holding his hand was relaxing. She felt fuzzy inside as a million different questions came to mind. Did this guy have a girlfriend? She hoped not, that would be rude of him to hold hands with a random girl if he did have one. Where did he live? How old was he?

"What's your name?" she asked, wanting an answer to the simplest of her questions.

"Mark? Maaarrrkkk? Where are you?" someone's voice said in the distance. Isabella was still looking at the water before turning her head in the direction of the noise. She looked back at the boy who was still holding her hand as he stood up.

"Over here," the boy said. Isabella panicked with embarrassment. She dropped his hand before taking a step away from him.

"Your name is Mark?" she asked, trying to make up for her rude act.

"Yeah." the red-haired boy said with a sad smile.

The girl plastered a grin on her face, trying to lift the mood. "I'm Isabella" she said with a small bow. She heard the familiar rustle of leaves behind her and turned around.

"I'm sorry man, I didn't think you'd get that mad." a boy with a thick silver chain and several rings adorning his fingers said. He broke his gaze on his friend and looked at the girl. "Who is this?" he asked with a wink and a cheesy grin.

"Isabella," Mark said the girl's name. The new boy wriggled his eyebrows at the taller boy.

"I'm Jackson," he told her. She bowed a little and said a faint hello. Jackson turned back to Mark to finish apologizing when Isabella felt her phone vibrate. She pulled it out and saw a text from her mother. It contained a list of things the woman wanted her daughter to buy for their dinner. She didn't notice the boys had stopped talking.

"Sorry, that was my mom. She's making me go get some things from the market. It was nice meeting you two." she said with a nod at each of them. Mark was a bit stunned with his lips still tugged downwards. You could almost see the light bulb appear above Jackson's head.

"We'll come with you." he said with a smile as he turned to her and looped his arm through hers.

"It's okay, you don't have to." the girl said, not wanting to waste either of their time.

"We can help you carry it back to your house. There's a store close to where you live, right?" Mark said as he joined them. He started leading the back to where they met, Jackson dragging her along

"That's not a bad idea." she whispered to herself.

"Maybe we can convince your mom to let us stay for a meal. I'll help her cook." Jackson said, happy with his arm still locked with Isabella's.

Mark scoffed, "You can't even make ramen."

Jackson shrugged as Isabella sighed. They were back at the bush. Mark had weaved himself through the branches and stood on the other side. Jackson removed his arm from hers and threw himself into a chauffeur's position.

"Ladies first," he said with a false serious expression. Isabella cracked a smile at this and wiggled through the leaves to the yard on the other side. Jackson made it through last and the girl looked at the worn out shed in the distance. She hoped her father wasn't looking through the window right now. She had friends over before, but never guys. So she wanted to put off that awkward interaction for as long as possible.

"Where were you off to? And with boys?" Isabella heard come from the back of her home. She groaned, which made both boys laugh a little. She couldn't put it off forever. They walked towards the woman who had one hand on her hip. Before the girl could open her mouth to explain herself, a voice beside her spoke up.

"Hello Mrs. Isabella's mom. I'm Jackson." he said with a deep bow "This is Mark" he pointed to his friend who was now bowing. "We're Isabella's friends, we live down the road."

This made Isabella scrunch her eyes in disbelief. The only houses 'down the road' have quarter-mile walking distance between each one. Why were they wondering all the way down by her house?

"Also," Jackson said, glancing at Isabella before looking back at her mother. "Isabella wanted me to ask you if it's okay for us to stay for dinner." he said as Isabella glared at him. The boy flinched, expecting her to hit him. "We are going to buy the food with you. You should at least offer to feed us." he said, standing straighter.

Isabella looked over at Mark and saw him pull a quick pout. Not him too.

"It's fine with me. Just make sure to get everything on that list I sent you." the mother said as she handed Isabella some bills for the groceries. Both boys gave the woman a quick bow as the girl started off for the store.

After a twenty minute walk, they arrived at the shop. During that time Jackson lead the way, narrating the imaginary lives of passersby. Mark tried to grab Isabella's hand once again but she kept avoiding it. Setting foot in the building, Jackson grabbed a cart.

"Mark, get in." he said to his friend. Mark shook his head and said he's good.

Determined to push someone around the in the four wheeled contraption, Jackson switched targets. "Isabella, get in the cart." he said.

The girl had no time to respond at she felt a pair of arms wrap around her waist and lift her into the basket. She turned to look at the culprit, just seeing a grinning Mark wink at her. Isabella let out a huff of air and reached for her phone.

"You don't have a passcode." she heard Jackson say from behind her. He handed the phone to Mark and started pushing the cart. "It's like shoving a mountain of potatoes." Jackson groaned.

"I'm an adult, and how did you get my phone?" she said, reaching for the device only to have Mark pull it away from her.

"How old are you." The red haired boy asked while scrolling through something on the phone.

"Nineteen." she answered.

"Psh, you're a baby." Jackson said as he glanced at the screen in Mark's hand, awaiting some direction.

"Well how old are you?" she asked. They didn't looked much older than her. What if they were pedos with tons of plastic surgery to make them look young? Her mind start wandering in crazy places when Mark spoke up.

"I'm twenty two. Jackson's twenty one. You are a baby getting pushed in a carriage." he said as he switched places with Jackson, handing the latter the phone.

The girl nodded at this. "Can I have my phone?" she asked.

The raven haired boy walking beside her lifted the device. "No" was all he said as they stopped in a pasta aisle to grab some of the listed items.

She threw her head back at looked at the two boys coming back to the cart. They handed her an item or two and placed the rest around her. She couldn't pretend she wasn't enjoying this though. It must have been a decade since the last time she rode in the cart at a supermarket. Maybe these befriending these two guys wouldn't be the worst thing in the world.

CHAPTER 7

It was now Mid-May and Jeremy felt that something was off. The village was in the center of a huge deserted forest on the edge of a not-so-huge town. The woods do have a few civilian houses lining the borders. Past those few houses, the area grew more urban and full of unsuspecting humans. As if the humans had anything to worry about.

It wasn't rare for werepeople to travel into the city. That's how most of them made a living and where the bought the things they needed. Having such similar DNA, they looked the same as any member of the foreign society. It was only once a month that the group became beasts.

There was no real reason for any of the werewolves to have an interest in the homes. So when Jeremy felt the urge to lurk around a specific house on his way to work, he was a bit confused. Werepeople have never wanted to eat humans or harm them in any way. He was also a human right now, so he wasn't afraid of some tragedy happening. It's just that his kind had no need to interact with humans unless it was essential.

Wanting to figure out the odd feeling, he followed his intuition. The boy was lead to the edge of the forest. A bush blocked his view, so he pushed back a branch. What he saw before him was a house loaded with cardboard cubes and furniture. He could see some movement through the back windows. Humans were moving into a nearby house, big deal. The boy was not satisfied with this answer and his inner wolf would not allow him to leave. He stalked around the side of the property, still hidden by the foliage.

He was much further from the house but had a clear view of its side and a bit of the front door. Jeremy could see an older man close up the back the moving van. There was a cluster of people, a family. Across the yard from the older man was a woman of the same age yelling things at him from the front door. He assumed these were the owners of the house and also the parents. A young man with an arm around a woman holding a baby, the son and his wife and grandchild. Another adult around his age, but female. She was laughing at him as she carried a lamp, the older sister. Behind them, a girl carrying a box and shutting a car trunk with her elbow. The prettiest girl he has ever seen.

Jeremy had to grip the plant in front of him to prevent himself from bolting to her aid. He wanted so bad to take the box from her and introduce himself. To be one of those nice boys all the girls have crushes on like in the dramas. But his inner demon was yelling at him to tackle the girl and pin her down. Stare into her eyes and make her feel the love the moon assigned him to have for her. He couldn't do either, the conflict spinning in his mind resulted in a headache. The anxiety the new thoughts gave made him almost want to run away. Nonetheless, she turned her attention to the trees behind him and surveyed the area. He couldn't keep the grin off his face when her eyes hovered over the bush he was behind.

The boy took a deep breath and kept his focus on the girl. It was still morning and he could call in late for work. Watching his mate seemed a lot more productive.

CHAPTER 8

Half an hour later they left the store with all the needed ingredients. In Jackson's left hand was a bag filled with junk food that he deemed necessary for the trio to try. Both boys had a bag in each hand while Isabella had a single plastic sack in her left. She was reaching for Mark's pocket with her right. The last time she saw her phone was in his grasp, now she could see the device's outline on his pocket. Both boys didn't want to give it back to her, whatever reasons they had were still unknown. If only she could pull it out with him noticing and return it to her own pocket. She was trailing behind the two by a few feet. They whispered about something Isabella didn't care about. She was too concerned on her mission.

"I've never seen this girl before today, why does she smell so familiar?" Jackson asked once he made sure Isabella was in her own world. Making her think neither of the boys saw her pining for her phone in Mark's pocket.

"I knew you noticed it. That's why you were so chummy from the get go, huh." Mark said.

"At first I thought you had finally found your mate. Until I realized that wasn't your scent." Jackson said.

"I didn't run off earlier just because you pissed me off." Mark started, pausing as Jackson tilted his head down and gave give a goofy look. He could sense Mark's lie. "Okay, I did. But I ran in front of her house without thinking of it. I thought it was the pull at first, but then she got close and I knew that couldn't be her own scent." Mark finished, eyebrows inching towards each other as he recalled the confusing situation.

"Do you think another wolf claimed her? She's for sure a full blood, there's not a trace of beast anywhere in her. What's a human doing smelling so...not human?" Jackson thought aloud. He kept his voice down due to the girl closing in on his friend's left pocket.

"Do you think she's someone's mate?" Mark asked as he sped up a bit. Wanting to keep the girl focused on her own task long enough for the two to figure out the scenario. Soon enough, the thought struck him. He and Jackson widened their eyes in sync. Mark smiled when Jackson became serious before speaking.

"Dude, Jeremy has a human mate, or, might kind of. Dude!" Jackson exclaimed as he stopped walking, causing Mark to do the same. Jackson walked over to the girl. She blew her cover and just stuck her hand down Mark's pants and pulled out her phone. Both boys were too caught up in their discovery to joke about what she just did. The girl just stuck out her tongue at the red haired boy when he looked at her. Jackson, now behind Isabella, started sniffing the girl. His eyes seemed to struggle not popping out of his skull after a few whiffs. The boy started pointing at the girl and mouthing 'Jeremy' to his friend. He was still behind and out of sight of the girl.

"What are you guys doing?" Isabella said when it had been a few moments of silence between the group.

Mark rubbed the back of his neck as the girl spun around to face Jackson. The latter pulled his hands together in front of him. He was still clutching two sacks of food while throwing on an innocent smile. "Nothing," Jackson said as he looked down at the girl, his chin reaching her eye level.

"So, how do you know Jeremy?" Mark asked. Isabella turned back to him with a confused expression. Jackson was yet again out of her sight and started shaking his head from side to side with a scowl.

"Who?" Isabella asked. The girl blinked a few times, curious about what had gotten into her new friends. With this, Jackson spoke up as he started walking again.

"He's a friend of ours, you'd like him." he said as looked back at the two, signaling them to follow him.

Five minutes later they were crossing the threshold into Isabella's home. The girl was now leading the two boys around the half packed living room and into the kitchen. Her mother was sitting cross-legged on the floor, watching a drama while folding clothes. The woman let the trio pass unscathed until she heard the rustle of plastic bags.

"Why didn't you take the reusable ones? Your father is going to have a fit if he sees those throwaway bags." Teresa yelled from her spot in the next room. Isabella let out an annoyed sigh. This being one of the few times she forgot a way to help the earth instead of destroy it. Both her and her father were massive science nerds. That came with a few repercussions of cleaner and smarter living habits. The girl bit her lip, still bothered by her mistake.

"Sorry, I forgot," was all she could yell back to her mother. She soon followed Mark's lead of unpacking the groceries. Soon the taller boy held all five bags in one hand. He looked at her with a raised eyebrow. "Just throw them away I guess. There's a trash can on the side of the house. My dad might see them if you use the one in here." she told him. He let out an okay and she told him thanks before he left to carry out the task. Isabella noticed Jackson had disappeared.

The girl looked all around her until she heard laughing from the next room. She walked in to see her mother laughing and the boy sitting next to her on the floor. His face held a playful seriousness while commenting on the actors before them. This caused another wave of chuckles to come from the woman. Teresa calmed herself as her laughs ended and handed a few articles of clothing to the boy. He didn't even complain before he took the t-shirt and folded it. He reached over for another while adding it to the pile already created in front of them. This made the girl smile and roll her eyes before she turned to go back to the kitchen.

She jumped at the sight of Mark right behind her. The boy just looked down at her and let out a small laugh at her reaction.

"Excuse me, what did you have in mind for dinner?" Mark asked, directing his voice to the woman. She turned around and let out an 'oh' as she got herself up. Jackson jumped up and made sure she didn't struggle. He even offered his arm for support.

"Thank you, but I'm not that old yet." The woman said as she walked into the kitchen. Upon seeing the things she asked for with a few foreign items, she turned to her daughter. "Do you mind making something from this? I'm a bit tired and your father seems to have a lot to do today." she said, not waiting for a reply as she went back to complete her housework.

"Sure," Isabella said before her mother was out of the room. Jackson went to follow in Teresa's footsteps. The boy stopped as Isabella snatched him back with her voice. "If you plan on eating then you should plan on cooking." she said while looking at the bill of his snapback sitting backwards on his head. The boy turned around and gave a small bow to the girl, even letting out a soft 'yes ma'am'.

The process of cooking dinner wasn't horrible. It just wasn't too pleasant either. Isabella was the only one who even knew how wash vegetables. The two boys provided well for moral support. Also chopping the vegetables after their head chef washed them. Over an hour of unsure actions and shoulder shrugs later, the meal was complete. The girl looked at the microwave display that read 5:53. She recalled eight hours ago, planning on having a simple investigation in the woods. Now she just finished cooking with two boys she just met in said woods.

Teresa walked into the kitchen and let a smile grow on her face at the food placed on the table. She watched as the young adults buzzed around the room. The three set up the table without a word between them. It reminded her of how she missed her eldest two and how nice it was to have a fuller home. "Isabella, go bring your father in for dinner," the woman told her daughter. The girl nodded as she sat down the silverware and headed for the door. Once she was out of earshot, she looked at the two boys settling themselves into seats. They hoped the chairs weren't already assigned to one of the three family members. The woman smiled, satisfied that her daughter had already made new friends. It helped that they were polite seemed to come from nice homes. After a few moments of silence, the girl and her father appeared in the doorway.

"Well, who do we have here?" the man said upon seeing the two boys sitting at the table. The two just gave a slight bow at the man as he took the seat across from Jackson. Isabella took the chair across from Mark, the mother was already sat at the end. The girl spoke up and answered her father's question.

"This is Mark," she said, gesturing to the boy in front of her "and Jackson. I met them today, they helped cook dinner." she stated before digging into the food at the center of the table. Jackson raised his eyebrow as if to say 'that's it?'. Mark copied her action and took some of the food into his mouth.

The man just let out an accepting grunt and looked at his wife. The woman was bowing her head in prayer before she ate. She was the only member of the family to be religious. Her husband always respected it enough to wait for her to pray before eating. Jackson had noticed this interesting dynamic. The boy rushed to bow his head and clasp his hands, not having enough time to remove his hat as well. He peaked at the woman muttering some words before ending with an amen. The boy made sure to repeat the word a bit louder than she did and smile at her when she raised her head. The entire group was now eating and enjoying their meal. It was when the father had enough of the silence that he broke it.

"How old are you two?" he asked the pair sitting in front of him.

"Twenty-one" Jackson said between chews, too invested in eating to consider manners.

"Twenty-two." Mark said after making sure to swallow what was in his mouth before opening it.

"Are either of you still in school?" he asked, watching them stuff their face as if they hadn't had a proper meal in months.

"No sir, Jackson and I are both interns at a company ran by our friend's family." Mark said, clearing the remaining bits of vegetable from the salad bowl. Isabella tilted her head at this. She didn't expect the pair to do something that was so normal for people their age. They just seemed a bit more, eccentric, than your average intern.

"What kind of company is it?" the mother spoke up, now interested in the conversation. Maybe she could hint at the two to put in a good word for her daughter. She didn't want the girl to leave the nest, but some help with tuition bills would be nice.

"It's a law firm kind of. Like an agency of lawyers and people who do that kind of stuff. It pays well, and it belongs to Jeremy's dad." Jackson said, looking at the girl while wiggling his eyebrows in her direction. She scrunched her face in confusion. All she knew of this Jeremy guy was that her two new friends wanted to hook her up with him. But she had no idea why.

"Who is Jeremy? Is he your boyfriend?" The father asked after having caught sight of the look Jackson gave his daughter. 'No 'Isabella said a bit quieter than Jackson had said 'yes'.

"I think we should be going. It was nice of you to let us to stay for dinner." Mark said as he stood from his seat. He grabbed Jackson by the back of his hoodie at lifted him a bit so he would take the hint.

"Well of course, you boys did help with the shopping and the cooking. It was a pleasure having you boys over, feel free the come back anytime." The mother said as she got to her feet to follow the boys to the front door. The sun sat in the middle of the sky so daylight was still plenty. The man took note of this as he told the boys a quick goodbye and headed back outside. Isabella sat alone at the dinner table and stared at the empty dishes before her. Who were those boys and why did they insist on getting her with Jeremy?

CHAPTER 9

Jeremy and Jason were in the former's room, taking a much-needed break. Even though it was a Sunday, Jeremy got called into his father's office for most of the day. Jason was pretty energetic by nature. He would never turn down the offer of lazing around with his best friend. Playing video games was just a bonus.

It was around seven when Jackson burst through the door. Following him was Mark who gave the duo a smirk. Jason paused the game before asking

"What's that smell?"

This made Jeremy stared down the pair. Upon seeing what they were interrupting, the newcomers grabbed a controller and sat down

"You're such a creep you know. Isabella has no idea who you are yet she reeks of your scent." Jackson said as he turned on the controller to join the game.

"Who?" Jason asked the question Jeremy had in mind. The latter felt something click as he added it all together.

"Is that her name? Isabella." Jeremy pondered aloud, not focused on the game anymore. Just thinking about his future mate got his inner wolf excited. "Wait, is that what she smells like? Where were you two?" Jeremy asked as his paternal nature for his friends conflicted with his wolf's jealousy. Why did his friends smell like his mate and know her name? He had yet to have her acknowledge his existence.

"We had dinner at her house. Her parents like us." Mark said before turning his head to look back at Jeremy to add "a lot."

Jeremy lifted his controller and jerked his arm as if he was going to throw it at his friend. The red head laughed this off and faced the tv.

"But, why does she smell like, you know," Jason asked, still not filled all the way in.

"She's a human. That old lady from when we were twelve was right. Jeremy has a mate who won't leap into his arms the first time they make eye contact." Jackson said. This made Jason widen his eyes and drop his jaw. He stared at his friend who was becoming even more bashful.

"You should have told me about this." He said as he kept his eyes on Jeremy. The other boy just kept looking forward and nodded a few times, not wanting to talk about it. Jeremy knew that most humans reject their kind when they discover the wolf part. But that wouldn't make the boy lose hope. If he could just meet the girl and have her fall for him like any normal human relationship. Maybe she would be too attached by then to leave. He didn't know. He was still stuck on the best way to approach her to say 'hi'.

"She's nice and pretty, kinda quiet too. Perfect for you, only if you'd grow a pair and talk to her. Not just creep from a distance often enough that your stench clings to her." Jackson said before adding "You're lucky she didn't fall for Mark." he said then directed his speech at the boy next to him "I saw you flirting with her all night. What if she was your mate too? You are a red wolf after all." The boy finished.

"Shut up Jackson, don't joke about that," Jeremy said.

"So, Jer found his mate?" Jason asked, having learned so much about his friend in the past five minutes.

"And he's too shy to talk to her," Jackson said before letting the controller drop from his grip. Mark won the game.

"Why didn't you tell me anything, like at all?" Jason asked his friend, feeling left out.

"I don't know, it's weird," Jeremy mumbled, feeling embarrassed about it all.

"You know who isn't weird? Isabella's mom. I wonder if I can get her to adopt me." Jackson said as he let

Mark set up the next round.

"You already have a mother, don't try and steal mine. Where is your mate anyway? Doesn't she have parents that will become your in-laws?" Jeremy asked, gaining more confidence with the topics of mates and family. He just saw the boy in front of him shrug and whisper

"I don't know who she is yet."

"Why don't 'you help Jer get with what's her name. That way you wouldn't be so scared to find the girl you're destined for." Jason said, trying to mediate his friend's love lives. He already found his mate three years ago. He was in a long distance relationship with her right now. She was studying abroad in Japan for the semester. He had a lot of free time that he used to spend with her. So he was willing to dedicate himself to guiding his clueless friends. Even taking on the most difficult case himself. "And I can try to help Mark figure out why he's such a late bloomer," he finished.

The boys were half listening to what he said, but they all still let out sounds of agreement.

An hour passed and Jeremy heard Jason's stomach growl. As if on cue, Jackson's phone rang. He pulled out the device and saw the picture he took of the girl sitting in the shopping cart.

"It's Isabella," Mark said with a smile after seeing her name on the display.

"I knew it would be a good idea to put our numbers in her phone," Jackson said, proud that his efforts proved useful as he hit accept. "I'm with Mark so I'll put you on speaker phone," Jackson told the girl before she could say hello.

"Sorry it's so late," she said, Jackson looked at the time, it was only a little after eight. "But when I searched my phone to see what you two did, I found both of your numbers. So I thought it'd be okay to call," she started as Jackson looked at Jeremy. He grinned at the latter who looked love-struck at the sound of her voice. "Anyway, my mom had a fit when she saw all the stuff you bought. She liked to make use eat healthy so she started lecturing me. But then I told her it was yours and she said it okay. She even told me to invite you to watch a drama with or something whenever you're up for it. I'm pretty sure she likes you better than me. But you should come and get all the chips before my dad finds it and gains fifty pounds." she finished with a cheery tone. She giggled when she said her mom preferred Jackson over her own daughter. Which, could be true.

"We're with a couple of friends right now, but we'll be over there soon. Ask your mom if she watches It's Okay, That's Love. I'm still on episode four." Jackson said, set on taking up the offer of watching a drama. The girl laughed at this, making her two new friends smile. The sound just tugged at the heartstrings of the boy who the moon made fall in love with her.

"Okay, I'll tell her you're coming. Just knock at the front door and she should let you in." the girl said, hanging up before Jackson could reply.

"She sounds cute," Jason said.

"She is cute." Mark confirmed as he stood up and placed his controller on the table behind him. Jackson mimicked his actions as the other two didn't make a single effort to move.

"Well, we don't have all day. Let's go meet your

future girlfriend." Jackson said as he pulled at Jeremy's wrist to get the boy up.

The boys took the path straight through the forest. The groups noticed an older man letting out noises of frustration from the shed.

"That's her dad I think. He's nice but kind of tough, not tall either." Jackson said, describing the man to the ones who haven't met him yet. The boys went around the side of the house to see the porch light was on. Instead of knocking, Jason buzzed the doorbell. After a moment of silence, Jackson went ahead and knocked.

"I guess it doesn't work." Jason murmured to himself.

A second after Jackson's knock, the door opened to reveal the older lady.

"Come on in boys, it's nice to see you again." she said as she stepped out of the way to let them all in. They took turns saying hello a giving a quick bow when they passed the woman. Once everyone was inside, Teresa closed the door and looked at the group before her. "I know Jackson and Mark," she said, gesturing to the familiar boys " but who are these two?" she asked, keeping the warm tone in her voice.

"Ah, I'm Jason and this is Jeremy." Jason said as the pair bowed yet again.

"Jeremy," she said, recalling the name from dinner. "Didn't you mention he's a lawyer of his father or?" the woman asked, directing her question at Jackson.

"My dad owns a law firm. I usually just assist him when he needs me. I'm not interested in becoming a lawyer, but he plans on me taking over the company some day." Jeremy spoke up, wanting to make a good first impression. The woman just nodded her head and went back to her spot on the couch.

Jackson almost skipped over to the spot beside her. Mark rolled his eyes and went into the kitchen to look for the snack they left behind. Unsure of where else to go, Jason and Jeremy followed Mark into the next room. They saw Isabella searching through the pile of snack sat on the counter. The girl must have seen them from the corner of her eye because she jerked away from it. She let out a sigh of relief when she saw who it was.

"Sorry, I thought you were my mom." she said while going back to her digging for something appealing. "I had to wait until you guys came so Jackson could distract her for the coast to be clear. Please don't tell her I'm eating this junk." she said as she held onto a bag of candy and looked Mark dead in the eyes.

The boy just laughed and said okay before introducing the two strangers. "This is Jason," he said, pointing at the tallest of the three "and this is Jeremy." he finished, pointing at the boy who rivaled Mark in height. Isabella just smiled at them.

"Nice to meet you, I'm Isabella. I have to go finish a project, so see you later." she said directing the last part more to Mark than the strangers. One of whom looked like he was having a stroke.

"Oh, maybe we can help you. Jer and Mark are smart." Jason said, patting his stiff friend on the back.

"Why are we smart?" Mark asked, wondering why Jason had thrusted the chaperon roll onto him.

"Because you two graduated with straight A's. While I would much rather eat snacks and watch tv." Jason said as he grabbed a few bags from the pile and made way back to the living room.

"He seems nice." Isabella said while leading the two back to her room.

"Sometimes," Jeremy said as he gained back his ability to speak. She didn't seem affected by his presence, which hurt. The boy was struggling to keep himself from pouncing on her. His inner wolf was screaming to do just about everything he shouldn't do. 'Your mate is right there, you should be right there too. Why are you so far away, go, go goooooo it screamed at him. Jeremy just did his best to brush it off and put on a well composed smile.

The three walked into the girl's room. It had four white walls and a bed next to the not so large window. A dresser was beside the window and a small table next on the bedside. The only thing on the walls was a rather large Super Junior poster. Mark had one foot in the room as before he came up with a reason to leave.

"I have to use the bathroom," he said and turned out of the room. He didn't even pretend to need directions. The boy just walked down the hall and joined everyone in the living room.

This made push her eyebrows together in confusion. Her room was even all the way unpacked and it scared him off. She just shrugged at his oddness and on her spot on the floor in the sea of her school work.

Jeremy was still taking in the room and the overbearing scent it held of the girl. He saw the poster and it made him smirk. Before he could think better of it, his mouth let out what his mind was thinking. "How old are you to have that up?" He asked, pointing to the image too many pretty boys squeezing into one setting.

This made Isabella look up from her work and follow to where he was pointing. She couldn't care less if people joked about her taste in music. It was what she liked, not what they liked. If other people saw it as immature, then she didn't mind seeming immature. "I'm nineteen, how old are you?" She asked, looking the boy in the eyes.

He didn't return the gaze as he cleared his throat, feeling a bit awkward. "I'm twenty-one."

"Noted." was all she said before collecting the papers she needed to finish her project. "Are you good at science, oh-so-wise twenty-one year old?" she asked.

CHAPTER 10

Isabella was now in her room, finishing her biology project. Helping her was the boy her new friends had been trying to set her up with. Having known him for ten minutes, he didn't seem horrible. But for some reason, she felt comfortable with him. Whenever she made new friends, she felt as though she had to be nice and not too playful. That was at least until they've known either other for a while. But the second she noticed Jeremy, she felt relaxed. It was like they were already best friends. So she didn't felt out of place teasing him. It almost felt like she needed to assert dominance over him. This was something she never experienced or even thought of doing before. She was the type of person to get nervous giving her opinion during group work at school. She could never see herself as being authoritative in any sense.

"Not like that, write it higher," she said, reaching to take the marker out of his hand. He just held it out of her reach as she went on to point to the poster "Put it up here," she directed.

The project itself needed to be an essay and a twenty-minute presentation. For the second part, she chose to do a poster as a visual aid. It was a group project that she had the luck of getting stuck with doing most of the work for. She was writing the important parts on the board for her not so smart members to read from.

"Here, you write it, you have better handwriting than me." Jeremy said as he gave her the marker. She took the marker and started copying the information. After half a sentence, she paused to look at what to put next. "Oh no wait, nevermind. You don't have better handwriting than me." Jeremy said as he reached to take the thing from her grasp. The two had ended up sitting across from each other with the board between them. But when the girl heard him say this she rolled her eyes and stood up from her spot. He didn't flinch when she moved onto the bed, taking her laptop with her. "What am I supposed to write?" he asked.

"I think I'll make a powerpoint instead." the

girl said from where she lay on her stomach above him. He looked up at the screen and saw her opening a new slideshow and he let out a sigh. He closed the cap on the marker and grabbed the papers he thought would be important. Even though he had no idea what the project was even covering. The boy walked over the empty side of the bed and flopped down next to her.

"Here," he said as he laid the papers between them.

"Thank you," she said as picked out a template for the slides and reached for the stack. He wiggled closer to her and tilted his head beside to hers, being nosy in what she was doing.

"I leave for ten minutes and you two are all over each other." Mark said as he walked in the room with three cans of soda. He tossed one at Jeremy, who caught it midair. He laid the other unopened one next to Isabella.

"We're working," Jeremy said as he opened the drink and took a sip.

"I'm working," she said, putting emphasis on

the first word. "you're just" she paused as she thought of what to say "existing," she finished.

"I do that pretty well, don't I?" he said more than asked as he looked at her, returned with her making an annoyed face at him. He imitated her before pulling back with a smile and taking another sip of his drink. Mark was standing next to the two and just watching how they got along so well. But weren't being too physical or affectionate about it. It was a different first meeting than he has ever seen from any other set of mates. But then again, only one of them is a werewolf. Mark was soon pulled from his thoughts.

"How did you even get these?" Isabella asked, holding up the can of soda, reading the nutrition label.

"Jackson asked your mom for some comfort food. She went and grabbed these from your dad's stash." Mark said as he took the drink from her and cracked it open before giving it back.

"My dad has a stash? No wonder he's so fat when all mom's cooking is super healthy." the girl said before taking a mouthful of the drink, followed with a burp. She covered her mouth with her free hand as her eyes bulged in embarrassment. The boys just laughed at her actions and shook it off. "I don't want this." she said, handing the drink back to Mark.

"You sure? Seemed like you liked it a lot." He said as a slight tease, chuckling as he took the can from her and sat it on the small table next to him. The girl ignored him and started typing, transferring the information onto the presentation. Mark looked at her screen and then at Jeremy. The latter seemed entertained with watching her fingers move across the keyboard. "Do you need any help?" he asked, ready to leave the room.

"I'm good, thank you," she said, her eyes never leaving the display. Jeremy looked up at his friend, only for the redhead to smirk at him. The coal haired boy gestured at his friend to get out. Mark let out a silent laugh as he left the room. "Just remember to use protection." he sang out from a few steps down the hall. This had Isabella raise her head, glance at the door and then turn to the boy beside her.

"I have no idea what he's talking about," he said. The girl narrowed her eyes at him, which caused him to give her an eye crinkling smile.

After an hour of silence, the girl checked over her work for the third and final time. She let out a sigh and saved it. "Finally finished," she said as she saw the time was now 10:27. The girl looked over at the boy who fell asleep after not having moved for so long. Isabella never noticed he had been letting out soft snores every few seconds. They must have faded into the background since she was so into her work. Not caring that they just met, she slapped his shoulder to wake him up. The snores stopped but the boy didn't move. She moved in closer to look at his face and check if his eyes were open. The girl squeaked as two arms wrapped around her, crushing her body against his.

"I'm sleeping," Jeremy whined in a rough voice with his eyes still closed. The girl's head crammed under his chin as he rolled a bit more to keep her from moving. She lower her head while wiggling to try and escape. But he let out a whimper identical to that of a puppy. She could imagine the pout on his face.

"You have to wake up and go home. I finished my homework." Isabella said, remembering his three friends who she hadn't seen in a while. "I think your friends might have left without you." she said, giving up on breaking free and now trying to use logic.

"Good, now I can rest in peace," the boy mumbled into her hair, his face buried into the crown of her head.

"You're not dead, yet. But you will be if my parents walk in." she said, trying to scare him. This just made the boy loosen his grip enough for her to roll away. Isabella hopped off the bed and glanced at Jeremy. He was now laying on his side, looking at her with a hint of a smile. She just let out a playful scoff and left the room to see what happened the others. She heard him behind her when she reached the end of the hall and peered into the living room.

Straight across from where Isabella stood was the front door. Beside that was the television. Opposite the tv was the couch to her left where the three boys sat. Jason was leaning on the far armrest sound asleep. On the other end Mark sat with his eyes glued to his phone. Between the two was Jackson, sitting with both feet planted on the floor. He sat whispering commentary to himself about what was happening during the show. From behind her came Jeremy, walking over the group. He picked up an abandoned bag of chips that were resting on the table in front of them. He squeezed himself in the middle of Jason and Jackson. The caught Mark's attention and he raised his head to look at the newcomers.

"Does this mean we can leave now?" Mark asked.

"Shhh! This is intense and I lost the remote so I can't pause." Jackson whispered to the boy beside him. He also realized his awkward stance and sank back into the couch. The boy pulled his legs up and threw them across Mark's lap. This small interruption must have woken Jason. The remote appeared in the boy's hand as he passed to it Jeremy. Jackson didn't see this happen, so his jaw dropped when the screen in front of him froze.

"Why are you all still here? Where did my mom go?" Isabella asked the boys, tired and wanting them to leave.

"Mrs. Teresa went to bed early. She said it's okay if I wanted to spend the night. I didn't leave so no one else did either." Jackson said, wanting to turn his drama back on.

"You guys can't stay the night." Isabella said, not caring too much about what they did anymore. But she couldn't let four boys stay in her house overnight, also having just met them today. She didn't think they were sketchy in any way shape or form. But she wasn't idiot enough to consider letting strangers spend the night.

"Your dad even came by like twenty minutes ago and said it's okay as long as we sleep in here." Mark said, not wanting to move from his spot.

"Yeah, even your dad said it's okay, and he's kinda scary. So it is okay for to stay, alright. Goodnight." Jackson said, his fingers itching to hit the play button. Isabella let out a sigh and headed back to the comfort of her bed. If they wanted to stay, then they could stay. But if they were lying and got caught, she wasn't taking the blame. When she tried to close her bedroom door, someone pushed it open. "Jeremy, get out." she said to the boy standing before her.

"Are you going to make me sleep on the floor. With them?" He asked, pointing down the hall.

"Yes," Isabella said as she put a hand on the door, an inch above the knob, and tried to close it. He still held on and forced it open again, now taking the liberty to walk in her room.

"But what if I have to work tomorrow? I can't sleep on the floor and be all professional and lawyer like the next day." He said, looking at her and giving her puppy dog eyes.

"Here," she said, walking past him and opening up her closet door. Inside were all her unopened boxes that she didn't feel like unpacking yet. "Come grab this," she said to the boy while pointing at a medium sized box on top of the shelf. He came over and got the box down, handing it to her since it was pretty light. She sat the box on her bed and opened it up. Inside was a spare comforter and two pillows. She pulled them out and gave it Jeremy. "Now you won't be cold when you sleep on the floor." she finished with a forced smile, proud of herself for coming up with a solid solution.

"By myself?" He said as she guided him down the hall. "But I'm a guest, you should be kind enough to spare your bed for me." he said as joke when she took the blanket from him and spread it out on the floor in front of the tv. From the couch Jackson was squirming, trying to see the screen from behind the two. Jason was trying his best to stay awake. But he gave up when the tv disappeared and he had nothing for his eyes to focus on. Mark was content scrolling through social media on his phone. This being his normal before bed routine that he could do from anywhere.

"I'll sit with you until you fall asleep you big baby." Isabella said as she yawned, giving up her argument due to the exhaustion falling over her. She sat down on the thick blanket. Jeremy did the same while handing her one of the two pillows. Isabella placed the pillow on her left and layed down sideways. Jeremy took this opportunity and laid behind her, setting the pillow under his head. He threw an arm around the girl as they laid down and watch the drama through heavy eyelids. The girl rationalized a plan for if she should wake up to a parent fussing over what was going on. She would just blame Jackson. It was all his fault if you thought about it. Her mother had already broken rules for the boy. Isabella figured the older woman would never dare punish him. He was like the new golden child of the family, and he wasn't even related by blood. Isabella calmed herself with this plan as she closed her eyes. She fell asleep to the beat of Jeremy's heart pressed against her back.

Mark's curiosity got to him as he looked to see what the pair had been doing. The boy saw the couple brave enough to already be cuddling in the middle of the living room. The eldest boy tapped Jackson with the back of his hand and pointed to the scene in front of them. Jackson paused his show and a genuine smile broke out across his face. The boy felt around for his phone. When he couldn't find it after a quick search, he settled for snatching Mark's. He exited whatever was pulled up and opened the camera. He angled to phone down to capture to sticky sweet sight below them. Jackson tapped the screen with his thumb. He admired his photography skills before showing Mark the image.

"I'm the best wingman ever," Jackson said while handing his friend the device.

"Excuse me, I'm the one who got them alone," Mark said as he looked at the picture and had mild envy. When would his mate show up?

"I think I did a lot more than you. You'll see when I set you up with your girl. You'll be thanking me for the rest of your life." Jackson said with a happy confidence. He was proud that he could make two of his friends happy by getting them together.

CHAPTER 11

Mark awoke before the sun had risen, but he wasn't the first. He looked beside him at a sleeping Jason hung off the couch. He would be rubbing his sore neck the rest of the day. Mark wanted get up and move him. But he knew his friend is a light sleeper and would not want to wake up to someone touching him. In front of him the girl was asleep on the floor by herself. Where had the other two gone? Mark got up and stretched his legs before wandering into the kitchen. He wanted to check the fridge but decided against it. It wasn't his house and in reality he shouldn't have stayed the night. It was late and nothing made sense. All the boy could remember was a few stupid hashtags he spent an hour reading tweets about. When he turned to go back in the other room, he saw movement from the back window. The boy walked over the door and heard hushed yelling.

"Are you serious, wasn't Mark freaking out on you yesterday enough?" A voice said. Mark remembered what happened the day before. The thing that got him mad enough to run away. He didn't wait for Jackson's reply as he opened the door to face the boys.

"If you are still thinking about fighting them, then you need to stop." Mark said as he stepped out on the porch.

"Dude, it's not just us anymore, look," Jackson said, pointing to the dead squirrel. Mark hadn't noticed he was lucky enough to step over it earlier.

"Why, what, it stinks," Mark said, confused about what it was doing there.

"Yeah man, it smells like shit because it's coated in their scent. How did they even know about her? Now they're going to torment her too. She's human, she has nothing to do with this." Jackson said, trying to keep his voice down as he grew angrier at the situation.

"It's not cool, but what do you expect to happen? We barge in there, scare them and they'll stop?" Jeremy asked, trying to reason with his friend.

"Yes! We'll go over to their territory, fuck with them a bit and make them get the message." Jackson said, his voice growing higher.

"No, idiot. If we did that it would just cause even more problems. You do realize they are still bitter from a hundred years ago. Sure, it doesn't make sense why they're acting up now. But if we try to" Jeremy said before Jackson cut him off.

"Bitter? What does The North have to be bitter about? They should be grateful towards us. Our ancestors made them see reason when they were going insane. They should feel blessed that we didn't ship them off to the real North Korea." Jackson said, his voice dropping as he yawned after his statement.

"It's messed up that they wanted a monarchy that held absolute power over everyone. But we weren't nice about it either. Did you even pay attention in the history courses from our ancestors? We recruited help from humans, humans who had real weapons. On top of that, we made a deal that when they helped us, they could keep the corpses. Do you remember the number of how many werewolf bodies they gathered to pick apart? Two hundred and thirty-seven. Do you remember how many members The North had when we first separated? Fifty-four. Our ancestors almost wiped them out. Do you remember how many-" Jeremy said before he got cut off.

"Shut up," Jackson said, not wanting to hear it.

"Four. Jackson, four, The South only had four casualties. Sure, our side had less than a hundred members after the separation. But at least they didn't try to make us go extinct. I know if I was a part of The North, I wouldn't like us too much either." Jeremy finished.

"Fucking whatever Jeremy, okay. I get it, we are evil in their eyes. We are murders and we side with humans. We should feel bad and shit. But that's in the past and why do they care now." Jackson said. Mark just stood there and recalled the conversation he had with Jackson yesterday. The boy wouldn't listen to the redhead and things got heated. "A spineless fucking worm who would get crushed by any wolf in battle. Because of his mutant genetics that gave him disgusting orange fur." Is what Jackson called his friend. This got Mark so angry he thought he could feel the familiar snap of bones and he had to get away. He ran to release some of the anger. That's when he appeared in front of Isabella's house.

"Hey, yeah, why are they starting stuff here? Do they have spies lurking around our perimeter or something? Did they already figure out Jeremy has a human mate?" Mark asked. The boys looked at each other a bit unsure. Now have a few new theories popping in their heads. Before any of them could voice their ideas, the door cracked open.

"What are you boys doing out here so early?" Isabella's father, Henry, asked while looking each of the boys in the eyes. He soon scrunched up his nose and let out a disgusted sound before looking in front of his feet. "Again? Damn it, I better throw it away before Isabella sees this." The man said aloud to himself as he turned back into the kitchen.

"Did he say again?" Mark asked, vocalizing what the trio had been thinking.

The man stepped back out and picked up the dead body with a handful of old newspaper. The group of curious boys accompanying him to the trash can, now interviewing him.

"Excuse me sir, but did you say again? This happened before?" Jackson asked, putting on his angelic little boy front.

"Every morning since we moved in." The man answered as the boys looked at each other with wide eyes. "What were you all talking about earlier? And don't act dumb. I was on my way to my office, but then I heard you all out here yelling. Something about werewolves and the north and humans. Tell me, I won't bite." The man said, chuckling to himself at his last remark.

"Oh, it was nothing, just you know, a movie we watched last night. Intense war and wolves, scary stuff." Jeremy said, coming up with a flimsy excuse off the top of his head. The other two boys looked at the man, nodding at their friend's statement.

"I'm an ecologist, not an idiot. Some guys down in the x-rated area grew worried about werewolf disputes out here. I didn't believe them so they told me to investigate it myself, giving me no evidence. That's the reason I moved my family out here. You boys need to tell me everything you know about this. Otherwise, I'm going to get my wife's wrath on you three. And you." The man paused while pointing at Jeremy "For, well you know what you did. Don't think I didn't see you two last night." he finished. He alluded to how Isabella fell asleep in the middle of the living room in Jeremy's arms.

'Let's feed him bullshit 'Jackson expressed through his subtle nod at the other two.

"And don't think I didn't hear the word human and mate next to your name, boy," Henry spoke up. His eyes locked on the side of Jeremy's head, turned away from the man's hard gaze. "If you are my daughter's boyfriend, you need to tell me all about this mess. I wouldn't even care if you three and that other boy werewolves. As long as you boys behave well like you did yesterday, you could be demons from hell for all I care." The man finished. HIs logic thrown out the window at the idea of supernatural creatures being real.

Jeremy sighed and looked at his friends with sad eyes. "Let's just be honest with him, it'll make things easier if someone knew." he said.

Jackson rolled his head around before dropping it in his hands. The boy let out a long dramatic sigh. Mark just shrugged and nodded. Jackson saw this and kept up the hurt act as he said "Are you betraying me?"

Mark scoffed, "You made fun of my hair, of course I'm betraying you." he said before turning to look at the man in the face. "We'll tell you all about it. But, you can't let your daughter know, it could freak her out." he said as a small plea.

The man crossed his arms and squinted his eyes up at the boy who was a few inches taller than him. "I'll tell her what I think she has a right to know." he said before gesturing for the boys to follow him. "Come on, we'll talk in my office." the man said as he walked over the dirty old shed with a table and a single chair.

The sun was above the horizon but not quite in the sky. The boys stood around the small room. They were almost through explaining everything to the man sitting next to his 'desk'. At one point, the man asked for the boys to stop so he could get a notepad and tape recorder. They refused, even threatening to locate his stash and set it ablaze. This had the man glued to his seat, telling the boys to continue their story. They first told him the story of the war dated over one hundred years ago.

Their version of the tale was more so summary. It spawned when one of the most influential members started making hasty claims. Then he started giving himself and those close to him unfair power in the society. This made them appear greater or above others. Soon enough, a good chunk of the village starting following this guy. They even believed that he was fit to be in charge of all. The other werepeople saw the unjust in this and rebelled. This rebellion had the man furious and he declared a war. During the war, the self-elected ruler was the easiest target. This wasn't just because he kept the same submissive entourage nearby at all times. It was due to his gray fur. This gave him dark gray hair, even at his somewhat young age.

The village had all its important buildings and facilities located more in the north. Wanting to gain whatever defense they could, the rebels fled south. Leading them into the wilder unclaimed section of forest. But, there was a remote research lab located below the border of their territory. This is when The South made the historical deal with the humans of the research lab. At first, the scientist were skeptical. They still showed up to battle on the full moon per request of their new allies. The humans grew amazed at the warriors shifting into beasts before their eyes. The full moon was when werewolves are at their peak aggression and strength. It was obvious both sides would make their largest attack during that night. The South planned on having the humans help just a tad. When the scientists remembered the deal, they became a little trigger happy. The South's allies killed every wolf that showed up to battle that night. This resulting in the iconic death total of two hundred and thirty-seven. This being a number all werewolf children memorized in their history course.

After this, they told him about the current situation with The North. It started with petty crimes, stealing food, killing Southern's pets, nothing harsh. Over the course of the past month, it escalated to threats of attack. Even mentions of the disgrace The South should feel for not honoring their ancestors.

"By ancestors, they mean wolves. The North isn't awful, but still crazy. Every full moon they collect all the children and elders who are too old to shift. They gather along the outside of a massive dome made of chain link fence. Then, everyone who would shift gets inside and surrounds the centerpiece." Mark started.

"The centerpiece is an old crusty bonfire pit that is pretty big." Jackson said, wanting to make everything clear for the man.

"Yeah, like ten or eleven feet across." Jeremy restated.

"But they circle around that thing. Then their leader shows up. He takes hormones suppressors so he won't shift until an hour after everyone else. He lights the fire and the people on the outside start chanting a hymn. It's rumored that no one in The South knows the lyrics because they are darker than the devil. I'm not sure, I think that's just a rumor though. They start chanting a minute before midnight. By the time they finish, everyone inside has shifted." Mark stated.

"Except for the king." Jackson added.

"Yes, and through some kind of process, they choose a sacrifice to throw in the pit. Most of the time its just stereotypical wolf prey, like pigs or chicken. But every blue moon." Mark said before getting interrupted yet again.

"Like, the actual blue moon that happens every other year or so. " Jackson said, nodding for Mark to say the next part.

"They have a battle. I don't remember how they choose the contestants. But the loser gets sacrificed." Mark said.

"And they get mad at us for not doing rituals like that." Jeremy spoke up.

Henry nodded, taking all this information in. "So, you boys are werewolves?" he asked, knowing he was correct from Jeremy's slip up of saying 'us'.

The boys just gave slow, awkward nods. This made the man lean back into his chair and run both hair through his wild hair. "So, when you all asked about the dead animal earlier?" he asked, hoping they catch on.

"It smells like people of The North. We think someone has been spying on your family." Mark said in what he hoped sound like a confident voice.

CHAPTER 12

Isabella awoke to the sound of someone groaning. She opened her eyes and recalled her location. Then she heard the person behind her shift off the couch. The girl turned around and saw Jason look around while massaging the back of his neck.

"Do you know where everyone went?" he asked her. The girl shook her head and felt around the floor for her phone. She found it and hit the home button, the time read 8:23. Her first class began at nine and the bus ride to her university took around half an hour. She looked down at her t-shirt and sweatpants. Remembering the presentation she would have to give, she got up and went to her room. She knew how to drive but had yet to get her license. She put on a skirt and a somewhat nice top. After throwing her hair up into a ponytail and it was half past eight.

The girl texted her father to let him know she would take his truck to school. While putting her laptop in her bag, she felt a buzz. The man responded with a no due to the girl not yet having a license. Isabella ran out of the room and headed for the front door. She noticed Jason sitting idle on the couch.

"Do you have your license?" she asked the boy. He looked up at her and let out a yeah. "Let's go then." she said while unlocking the front door and leaving it open for him to follow.

After his initial shock of becoming her chauffeur, Jason followed Isabella's directions well. He was a fast driver and often let out annoyed sounds and glares directed at other drivers. He did get her to school in less than twenty minutes, which was perfect for her situation. She also gave instructions of where to leave the car keys after he went back to her house. Once he pulled up in front of the building, Isabella let out a fast 'thank you so much' and hurried out. She didn't look back as she gripped the single backpack strap on her shoulder. The girl checked the time and noticed it was five till nine. She hoped she could squeeze in the classroom before her professor locked her out.

After a successful entrance and an awkward presentation, her first class was over. Ten minutes later was her history course that let out at a quarter before eleven. She went to a cafe on campus and brought a drink and some fruit for her lunch. The girl headed over to the grassy knoll she often met up with a few friends. She arrived at her spot and saw three people sitting there, none of which she knew. She went to walk past them in hopes of finding an empty spot for herself when one of them spoke up.

"Hey are you Isabella?" one of the boys said when she was a few feet away. The girl looked at them and saw they were all staring at her. feel uncomfortable, she let out a soft yes and walked toward them.

"Sit with us, Jason texted us and said you went here too." another boy, who had his hair gelled up versus the other two having shaggy cuts, said. At hearing the familiar name, she figured they were friends of her friends. It wouldn't hurt to sit with them. She settled into a spot between the tallest and the shortest of the bunch. After a moment of silent chewing, the shorter looked at her.

"Are you Jeremy's girlfriend?" he asked, stuttering a bit on the last word as if he wanted to use a different term. This made the girl choke on her apple and place a hand on her chest.

"Brandon, you idiot, don't kill her," the taller one said to the boy across from him. The girl calmed herself and shook her head.

"Sorry, but uh, no. I just met him yesterday," she said. The boys glanced at one another at this. "By the way, why is everyone saying that? He's not awful, but Jackson and Mark were teasing me about it before I even met the guy." she said, feeling out of place with the situation.

"Don't worry about it. By the way, I'm Tyler," the tall one on her left said with a nod in her direction. "This is Steve," he introduced the boy across from her who had quaffed hair. "And that's Brandon," he finished with a gesture to the boy on her right. She didn't question why he called the boy by such a random nickname. Instead, she said a quick hello to each of them with a forced smile. The group fell into a comfortable silence as they all ate their lunch. Once Isabella finished her drink, she got up and walked down to a nearby trashcan. After throwing the things away, one of her partners from earlier came up to her.

"Hey, the professor said he needed to see you."

he said while standing in front of her, waiting for a response. She just looked at the boy and said okay. The corner of his mouth raised into a half smile and he gave her a nod before walking away.

Isabella returned to her spot to see the boys packing up their mess of food and half done homework. She grabbed her bag and slid it on. "It was nice meeting you guys, I have to go," she said before she bowed a bit and walked away. From behind her, she heard their goodbyes grow distance as she kept a casual pace. Her final class was at noon, she hoped this meeting would be quick.

The girl made it to the classroom and looked in the window of her professor's office. The light was on yet no one was inside. She opened the door anyway and stuck her head inside. When she turned her head to get a full look around, someone shoved her in the room. The girl lost her balance but stayed upright by a foreign grip on her right upper arm. Isabella heard the person behind shush her as their other hand covered her mouth. The girl's breathing grew erratic as she struggled to remember basic defense mechanisms. She tried to kick behind her and wriggle out of the person's grasp, not knowing what else to do. A second later she felt something slide into the left side of her neck. A cold flow of numb came from the entry and the girl felt herself grow limp. Her vision became spotted before fading to black.

CHAPTER 13

Jason returned to Isabella's house and walked through the front door. He waited until he could sit back on the couch before pulling out his phone. The boy composed a text to Steve explaining the situation with Jeremy's mate. He included that the girl went to the same university as the younger. The boy still had his eyes glued to the small screen when the older woman walked in the room.

"All the boys are out in the back if you'd like to join them." Teresa said to the lone boy who looked a bit lost being alone.

He just gave her a slight nod and let out a quick thank you before getting up and leaving the room. Once he stepped into the yard, he heard familiar voices from the old shed. He walked over and saw his friends with Isabella's dad immersed in a conversation.

"So what have your people planned? Is there going to be an attack?" The man asked.

Jason's eyes widened at this. The group had yet to notice his presence at the doorway. "What did you tell him?" he almost roared in disbelief that the others exploited information.

"We had to, calm down. He suspected us from the beginning anyway. He's a scientist at the lab, the one that helped us during the war." Jackson said rather fast, wanting to get back to brainstorming a plan.

"No sir, a few people like Jackson want to though." Jeremy answered the man's question.

"Well, we should! If we keep letting them do petty stuff, it will soon escalate beyond our control. Might as well get the second war over with sooner than later." Jackson said as his legs twitched to pace around the small area.

Jason crossed his arms and scoffed from his

spot at the entryway. "Not this again," he said. The window shattered as a bullet flew and traveled into the side of Henry's skull. The man fell forward and toppled onto the ground. The boys were so stunned and didn't notice four multi-colored wolves enter the shed. Their moving in shoved Jason into the room. The two red and single brown beasts shifted into humans. This left the biggest and only blonde animal alone in wolf form.

"If you don't want to die, you better come with us." the brunette spoke as all three pulled out guns.

"What the fuck, they shifted by choice, and with clothes on? Is this a dream? It's not even-" Jackson said before the red heads moved towards the group. This caused the pale wolf to growl.

"Follow us to The North and no one gets hurt." The brunette said as he remained cool and stared the boys down.

'Even though you shot an innocent human, we'll trust you. 'Jason thought to himself. He looked to his friends as the strangers came toward them and walked behind each boy. The criminals brought each of the boy's wrists behind their backs. They held them with one hand as Jason felt the cold metal of the gun pressed to his temple. He glanced at his friends through the corner of each eye. It seemed Mark hadn't blinked in an hour. Jeremy grew even paler as he glanced to the dead body on the floor. The pool of blood flooded on the concrete around the man's head.

From outside, someone's footsteps crunched the short grass at they approached the tiny building. The blonde shifted mid-stride to check who it was. Another gunshot rang while a woman screamed. A grunt came from the absent man before he returned carrying Teresa's corpse. He heaved it down beside her husband's lifeless remains. The blonde went over to Jackson and grabbed him in the same fashion as the other hostages. He led the way out of the shed as the other foreigners followed with tight grips on the boys.

"Let's get them in the van first. Then I'll go back and set the shack on fire." the tallest said in his gruff yet nasal voice. The men shoved the boys around the house to the driveway. Behind the still warm truck was a red van with a tinted windshield and no windows. Jason glanced at the license plate and repeated the symbols in his mind. They loaded the boys one by one into the back. Once the doors shut, Jason pulled out his phone and entered the code into his notes app. He hoped it could prove useful. Sunlight rained in from the front as a few doors opened. The three smaller guys climbed in the van. They kept the casual tone while continuing their conversation.

"Minseok said he and Zitao grabbed the girl, but they knocked her out just to be safe. Turns out she and Minnie had a class together." one of the redheads said with a chuckle from the middle row. There was no back row, that being why the boys were seat-less.

"I still don't get how he can deal with being around full-bloods for so long. He goes almost every day too," the brunette spoke up from beside him.

"Well, how do you think he has so many transfers? You can't be at the top of the ranks without a constant flow of naive humans. Just tell the idiots you're having a party with free booze and they come running. Most of them already tipsy if tells them to come later enough, making it easier to attack. I don't ever see you complaining when you leech easy targets from Minnie's gatherings." the redhead said as he held his phone in front of his face. The light illuminated a red spot on the side of his neck

"When is Yifan coming back, did he fall in or something?" the other redhead spoke up from the passengers seat. On cue, the driver's door opened and the blonde jumped in and started the car. They pulled out of the driveway and turned down the road. Jason strained to catch a glimpse of the smoke rising from behind the home.

CHAPTER 14

The first thing Isabella saw was the ground moving under someone else's feet. Next she realized her body was slung over the shoulder of someone tall. She tried to raise her head while her hearing returned to her collection of senses. When she heard bits and sentences she didn't understand, she went limp. The girl decided it was best to close her eyes and play along.

The sting from the left of her neck hurt less than the surge of adrenaline caused by fear. She tried to ignore what they were talking about and mark off this experience as not real. When she heard talk of wolves and mates for some reason she couldn't help but listen.

"Why don't we just bite her and add her to our collection?" The one carrying the girl said with a tinge of a Chinese accent. Isabella could feel the vibrations ripple through his chest, making his words more intense.

"It doesn't work on those set to mate with half-breeds. They don't take suppressants down there because they adore humans." a familiar voice said from beside them.

"So, are we using her as the offering next week?" the one carrying her asked, trying to make sense of the entire operation. They all slowed to a stop. Isabella didn't feel herself lowering to the ground as she hoped. Instead, she heard the Jergling of keys from the other man before he spoke again.

"No, if we did that then it would have no effect. The South doesn't even know one of their own has a human mate yet. If we killed her now, they wouldn't care. Instead, we had the others-" the sound of a metal door cracking open cut him off. He continued speaking as the entryway let out a metallic screech. "-to grab the boy. From what Yixing has told us, he was with three of his pack. They were at the girl's house, plotting an attack with her father. He was a scientist like they used last time. He said they-" Isabella felt herself moving again, into the room. They walked until she slid off the stranger's shoulder and onto the cold concrete. The other man kept talking through this. "-had to get rid of the old man and a female witness. Since he was with Yifan, Luhan and Jongdae, they had no problem getting all four boys in the van. They should be down here any minute." he finished.

Isabella was laying on her side with her eyes closed. She heard footsteps of the other man with a familiar voice. The sound grew farther and she guessed he had left. The girl tried her best to remain limp and motionless until the tall guy left. She felt the atmosphere shift as the guy sat down beside her. The girl was so confused and disoriented that she wanted to cry. She needed the guy to hurry up and leave so she could sit in silence and calm herself down.

"I know you're awake, and have been for a while." she heard the guy whisper. She felt a frown stuck on her face. "I don't know why you're here either." he said, vocalizing one of her million questions. He didn't seem threatening, at least, not right now.

The girl threw away her composure and opened her eyes. She rolled on her back and propped herself up and looked around the room. It consisted of cement walls and a massive metal door across from her, wide open. She saw a square of light between her and the exit. There must be a small window behind her. When she let out her breath, it was a sob. She couldn't hold in the mix of anger, confusion and loathing any longer. The girl brought her knees to her chest, laid her head on them and sobbed quiet tearful cries.

She didn't sense the stranger lifting himself off the ground. She also didn't notice the entrance of her four friends into the room with escorts. All she felt were two new yet familiar arms wrap around her. She felt like she should push them away, but she no longer cared. She was too scared and confused to even raise her head and see who the newcomer was. Her sobs gained sound and caused her chest to expand and contract unsteady. She felt the arms lifting her onto their lap and their chin settling to rest atop her head. Her whimpers stopped as she forced her mouth shut and held her breath. Her thoughts affected her actions. What if she was over reacting? What if they were talking about someone else's parents who got shot? What if they were just discussing the plot of a movie and none of what they said was real? She needed to calm down. This was all a dream. It was all fake and she would wake up soon.

Isabella kept her mouth closed while taking in air through her nose. Then releasing it from between her lips. She opened her eyes and saw light peeking from above her bare knees. She was still wearing a skirt. What if she was flashing everyone when that guy was carrying her? The girl wriggled out of the person's grasp. She sat and felt her bottom and made sure she wasn't showing anything. Looking ahead, the door was now closed. Jackson, Jason and Mark sat in silence with their backs against the wall left of the door. Jackson held his head in both palms, fingers running through his cropped black hair. The other two sat on either side of him, scrolling on their phones.

She looked to the right and saw Jeremy staring at her through heartbroken eyes. Before the girl could stand to further smooth out her skirt, the boy scooted over to her. He pulled her to his chest and whispered 'I'm sorry'. Then the boy turned them away from the entrance and towards the window. A few seconds later Isabella felt the wetness of his tears hit her hair. She wanted to ask what happened but didn't think he was in the mindset to answer. She let him hold onto her for a little while.

The girl couldn't let the curiosity eat away at her forever. Jeremy was no longer showing the cracks of his crumbling composure. Isabella raised her head, making him do the same. She looked into his red-rimmed eyes and felt so much sadness. She forgot many details of the conversation overheard earlier. So she was still a bit unsure why he was being like this.

"What happened?" was all she could manage to say. The way his lip quivered made her feel villainous and victimized at the same time. He took in a shaky breath and shook his head, unable to speak. The girl wanted to get up and try to pry some kind of information from the others. Jeremy's grip on her only tightened.

"Later" she heard him mumble "I'm tired," he said. The girl sighed at this but let him rest his head in the crook of her neck.

She had no idea where she was and the only people she knew were a group of boys she met yesterday. She found herself in a situation that only seemed to happen in cliche tv shows. They must've gotten the inspiration from somewhere. The girl remembered she had no idea what time it was. If what she heard earlier was false, then her parents would be freaking out if it was too late. She couldn't move due to the person wrapped around her. She soon realized she left her phone in her bag, which was not with her. The girl slumped in defeat as one of the other boys spoke up.

"I texted the others. Jer, they're alerting your dad and his men." Jason said while sliding his phone in his pocket and remained seated.

This had Jeremy raise his head and turn around, still not letting go of the girl. He let out a breath while rubbing his face with one hand. "This doesn't feel real." he said aloud.

UNLEASH THE BEAST

The girl looked over to the groups of boys and caught Mark's eye. The redhead stared at her for a second before breaking eye contact. Jason's gaze rested on the ceiling as if a magic spell was up there. She looked at Jackson who was looking in her direction but not quite at her. His breathing was heavy and his eyes looked wet in contrast to his mild scowl. Isabella spent a decent of amount crying and so had Jeremy. She understood if the always playful and happy Jackson needed to shed a tear right now. It was stressful for everyone and no one knew what was going on or why they were here.

Several minutes passed of no communication between the group. The door opened and six men standing in a small crowd appeared. At the front, Isabella could see someone who looked, wait. That was the kid who told her to go to the professor's office. He was in her group for biology. Did he set her up? After looking around the room, he spoke.

"You two, come on." he said while pointing to the couple. Neither of them moved as they stared at the group. Feeling overwhelmed from today's events, Isabella shocked herself by speaking up.

"You set me up." she said with a glare locked

on the short man in front with light brown hair. He quirked an eyebrow at this. Having known the girl as a classmate for the better part of a year, this outburst was unusual. "You told me to go the office, and then you kidnapped me. You dick, you even shoved all the work on me in class." she said as the cogwheels of her mind clicked a few uneven pieces together. She let out a deep sigh after saying this. She had many other things to vocalize but no longer felt the need to do so. The girl always thought if she was nice and quiet then she would have no troubles. Her current circumstance proved that theory wrong.

The two taller men walked over to snatch the pair. Isabella had her eyes locked on the floor, watching as their feet moved closer to her. Before they could bend down, the girl stood up while grabbing the boy's hand. "Let's go." she said as she walked to the entrance, tugging the boy along. She avoided eye contact with her former classmate. The short man didn't mind the attitude and turned to lead the way. The tall men were close behind the couple. This locked them in the pack of bodies in case they tried to make a run for it.

CHAPTER 15

The pair was escorted to attend a meeting between The North and The South. The Northern King wanted the lower district to reunite with his territory. This sparked a verbal battle between the two sides and no conclusion was ever reached. It was made known, that the reason behind the abduction was to get The South to communicate with The North. After the unsuccessful discussion, the group was freed, but not without hesitation from the King and his men.

"Those guys still have my bag. My parents must be worried and I can't even call them," the girl said during the car ride back to their district. The boys exchanged glances to one another at the reminder of her ignorance.

"We should go to your house first," one of the boys

spoke up. Jason caught this from the driver's seat and noted the new destination, turning around and heading towards the crime scene.

Once they pulled into her driveway, there was an eerie silence coating the property. They all got out of the vehicle given to them by The North as mild compensation mixed with wanting the foreigners gone as soon as possible. Getting out of the car, Isabella walked towards the front door. The boys stood in place, unsure what to do until Jeremy caught up to her and grabbed her hand. He gave her a sad smile as he lead her around the house and to the yard.

When the burned concrete slab appeared where the wooden shed used to be, Isabella started crying. "I heard them talking about what happened," she said while trying to breath back the tears "and I wanted to pretend it wasn't true," she said while a massive sob popped out against her will "but it was," she said, now not caring about letting the cries escape.

After a crying session that all of them contributed a few tears to, the girl was still shattered. Freeing her hand from Jeremy's, she took a few steps away from the group so she could catch a glimpse of them altogether, separated from her. Isabella closed her eyes and inhaled through her nose then released the air between her lips. She settled her thoughts into a few questions and opened her eyes. The boys stood still and sad before her.

"Tell me what happened," she said as her eyes glazed over the boys and focused on the tall trees behind them. The pause caused by the boys shifting their heads to look at one another frustrated her. She took another deep breath and cleared her throat. "Tell me everything I don't know. Otherwise when I call the police, I will give them all four of your names and claim you as the criminals." she said. Isabella was tired, so tired. And it was only Monday.

"We're werewolves," Jason said.

This caused the girl to stare him down with the blankest look she could conceive. Did they think she was an idiot? With another huff, she turned to her house and started for the back door. It was time to call the police. With her mind so set on drawing together the details to recite over the phone, she was caught off guard when a hand grabbed her upper arm.

"Please let me explain," Jeremy said with desperation and red rimmed eyes. Isabella stopped and looked at him, then at the other boys behind him.

"Okay," she said, willing to hear them out, even if it was all lies. The girl wanted to hear anything, believe anything, that would make sense of what happened over these past few days. She leaned against the brick of the house beside the door and waited. With this, they began to tell her the truth.

CHAPTER 16

Isabella stood and listened to the boys explain the divide in territories and the history between North and South. It seemed plausible. Then they started talking about how werewolves came to be and something about the moon. This is where the story started leaning more towards fantasy than reality and Isabella didn't buy it. The girl maintained eye contact with whoever was speaking, but began to drift out of their words and into her own thoughts.

This all seemed tedious and complicated, so it might have some truth to it. How did any of it involve her though? She befriended some strange boys from the woods, next day they're all kidnapped and her parents are killed? The latter part of that sentence still didn't seem real. Maybe this was all a prank. Her parents wanted to teach her a lesson about stranger danger or something and were dramatic about it? any second they could appear in front of her and things would be okay. Thats what Isabella hoped.

The girl wandered out of her inner monologue and focused on whatever Jackson was on about now. Something about mating. Isabella let out a sigh and rubbed her eyes before letting both hands fall to her sides.

"So what does this have to do with me?" she asked the one question she most required the answer to.

Jackson looked at Jeremy and saw his friend's tired sad smile. Jackson groaned at looked back at Isabella.

"Because your Jeremy's mate," Mark spoke up. All of the boys looked at him but with shock. They were a little relieved that he stated it so simple and with such honesty. Now Jeremy was the only one still worried what the girl would do next. His friends were preparing ways to console him since Isabella's rejection was inevitable.

The girl looked at the group and tried to sort her thoughts. These random boys she knew almost nothing about were trying to sell her on some made up mythology. She could deny it all, call the cops and shove them out of her life. Or she could play into it and try to figure out what happened for real. Isabella folded her arms and straighten herself up against the wall. She wondered how long they had been out here telling her this story. The girl looked at each of them in the eye. Jason was on the far right and seemed relaxed yet sad, with hands in his pockets and posture a little uncomposed. Jackson next to him looked out of breath, he was probably the one talking while she zoned out. Mark was looking at her as if he thought he knew what she would say next. Jeremy was on the left of them all. He looked as if he was ready to cry but trying his hardest to hold it together, looking at the ground and avoiding her gaze. If she was his mate as they were trying to claim, he seemed nervous about it.

Isabella looked at the leaves of trees behind them grow yellow as the sun was beginning it's descent for the day. From all the stories shes heard about werewolves, a mate was like a partner, a love interest. So they are saying that she is his destined soul mate or something. Maybe if she went along with all of this, and pretended to be his girlfriend, or mate, whichever they prefer, she could learn the truth of what was happening. Whether or not their wolf story was true, if she stuck around them and found out what kind of world they're apart of, maybe she could figure the real reason for her parents death and do something about it. But would that help? She was in school, had no job and her siblings didn't live too close. What would she tell them? Isabella decided to play into their game to see where it would lead her. There wasn't much else she could do.

"Okay," she said. This caught the boy's attention, excluding Jeremy. "Say I believe everything you've just told me," she said, looking at Mark and Jackson. Isabella couldn't see how the silly boys she spent Sunday with are now telling her all of this mess. "what's going to happen now?" she asked, not sure what else to say. THe pair stared back at her, taken aback, before glancing away and trying to come up with a response.

"What do you mean?" Jackson asked a bit hesitant after a moment of stressed silence.

Isabella's eyes went wide. She couldn't stand being nice anymore. She had to be honest.

"What do I mean? You all come out of the woods and hang out with my family and I. Then I get drugged at school and end up in some room. We come back to my house and my parents are dead. Next you tell me some fairytale about wolves and war and expect me to be okay with everything? My parents were good people, the best people, I loved them," she had to pause to take a breath and force back oncoming tears "and they're gone for no reason? Now I'm stuck with this house and college and student loans and no money and no one. What do you mean what do I mean? What do you all mean to do about cleaning up this mess after you've fucked everything up?" Isabella stated before catching her breath.

She was working herself up and speaking the hard truths out loud only made that much more real. The stress was piling up faster than she realized. The girl just wanted to go to school and become a scientist and be normal like her brother and sister. She didn't even know if she liked science, it was just something her father loved. Growing up, it was all she knew and all he would talk about so she wanted to talk about it too. Now she was on her own with no one to talk to.

"So you don't care that we're werewolves?" Jeremy asked, now looking at the girl. Isuel made eye contact with him and tried her best not to have a fit.

"You seem nice and all, but I don't believe you're a fucking wolf, okay," she said. The boy seemed to perked up at this.

"How about you come to our village and we show you it's real. We can help fix things, I promise," he said while taking the smallest steps towards the girl until he was just a few feet away from her. She didn't even think before the words came out of her mouth.

"Will I die?" she asked.

"No," Jeremy answered, a bit surprised by her boldness.

The girl decided she had nothing to lose. "Fine, lets go," she said.

Jeremy looked at his friends, who were stunned by how well the scene played out. They all gave him a look that translated too 'how did that happen? 'mixed with 'are you insane? 'and Jeremy just smiled. Isabella was through with waiting on them. She stared walking around the house and towards the car. Jeremy noticed and caught up with her, too relieved to even care about her arms being crossed so he couldn't steal her hand to hold. She said he was nice and she didn't reject him.

CHAPTER 17

The drive to their village was close to silent. Jason drove with Jackson in the passengers seat and Isabella between Jeremy and Mark in the back. The girl, too uncomfortable to face either boy so she could look out a window, opted for staring straight ahead and catching view from the dashboard.

"Your house, Jer?" Jason asked a few minutes into the ride. Jeremy let out an "uh huh" at this.

With everything pilling in Isabella's mind, she remembered she has no idea what day it is. Now with the sun having just set an it now being night, she probably has school in the morning. Not to mention finals the first week of June. Even with her good grades, she was a horrible test taker. If she could manage to pass her classes, then anything could be possible. The fact that she didn't know the time or date of have a phone was giving her anxiety. She started to think about asking someone in the car when the vehicle came to a stop. Isabella wished she knew how long it took to get here but it didn't feel long at all. The boys started getting so she followed suit.

"I texted the others, they should be here soon," Mark said as he walked behind Jason and Jackson up the steps to the house. If Jeremy wasn't right beside her, Isabella would have stopped and marveled at the home. It looked to have just two stories but was tall enough to hold three.

It had a flat roof appeared to be a perfect cube. That was until you caught sight of the left corner, which was indented to hold a small one story attached roof with a balcony atop it. The home was cream colored with windows taller than any of the boys, but seemed darker due to the mass of vines covering any given surface of the exterior. The fact that it was night didn't deter from the simple beauty, given the property was lit up with solar moon lights along the walkway. In addition to that, some of the rooms were lit up, making the interior visible from the outside. Even though there weren't away neighbors for a quarter of a mile, Isabella was a bit worried when Jason walked right inside without ever having pulled out a key to unlock the door.

Once inside, the house was even prettier. The theme seemed to be modern and clean as most everything she had seen so far was of a white or gray shade. But the plants hanging in small baskets from the ceiling in front of each window gave the room more of a comfortable feel. The boys went and spread out on the two couches while Isabella sat in the lone reclining chair to their right. The seat was so plush and relaxing, Isabella was fighting to not fall asleep.

Jackson found the remote and turned on the massive tv across from him. On his left, Mark sat on his phone, typing away as usual. Jason on the couch in the left corner seemed to be spaced out in his own thoughts. Jeremy stood up from his spot beside him and walked over to the girl. Once he got her attention, he just motioned towards the hall with a jerk of his head, hoping she would follow him. Isabella didn't miss a beat and made way for where he was going. Once she caught up to him, they were heading towards a staircase leading down and he grabbed her hand. She didn't mind this but was nervous as to what he was going to show her. The stairs were big and steep, leading into a dark space. With no banister she could see, the girl was more than happy to use Jeremy as a support. As she squeezed his hand tighter to keep her balance down the pitch-black never ending steps, he grew more ecstatic that she was his mate. He was happy that the lack of light kept her from seeing the obnoxious grin couldn't keep off his face.

Once they reached what Isabella assumed was the bottom, Jeremy led her forward a few steps and flipped a switch. As the room became visible, the girl was unsure of what was going to happen next. The area was big, but seemed to be a storage room. There were tables and chairs among other pieces of random furniture of every color, big boxes and bags filled to the top and tied off. All of this stuff were clumped together in mindless piles around the room, leaving thin empty trails that served as walkways. One thing she did noticed was that the ceiling was high. It was tall enough for her to need an at least eight foot ladder to climb to the top of to be able to stretch her fingertips to brush the ceiling. After her examination of the room, she looked at Jeremy, who was already staring at her.

"What?" she asked. He squinted his eyes at her, looked ahead of them at the piles of things, and back at the girl.

"Do you not see it?" he asked. Now Isabella was the one giving a confused look as she shook her head. "You must be too short. Here," he said while releasing her hand and crouching down in front of her "get on my shoulders," he finished.

Isabella had no idea how doing that would

help. She wanted to think of something to say, but gave up and played along. He grabbed her calves while standing up. Even with the added height, Isabella didn't see anything that stood out/

"What am I looking for?" she asked. With this, Jeremy started walking.

"Nothing, but now you're stuck," he said with a laugh while spinning around, making the girl dizzy.

"So, you don't have anything to show me at all?" she asked while resisting grabbing his head to keep her balance as he walked around the room.

"I do. But it won't happen until the full moon, which is tomorrow," he said while wandering around.

"What day is tomorrow?" Isabella asked, reminded that she had little concept of the current time.

"Wednesday," he answered.

That meant today was Tuesday. She missed an entire day of classes. At her university, six unexcused absences meant automatic failure in most of her classes. Today made the fourth in almost all of them.

"I have school tomorrow, what time is it?" she asked, now once again stressed out. Jeremy let go of one of her legs to fish for his phone in the pocket of his shorts.

"9:13. You can spend the night here, I'll drive you," he said while locking the device and putting it away.

"Those guys took my backpack and it had all of my books and notes and my phone and everything. I don't think I could go to class or do homework even if I wanted to," she said with a sigh.

"Really? I'll ask my dad if can do something," he said. Isabella rolled her eyes. She had no clue who this guy's father was, but she doubted he could do anything. Nonetheless, she kept this to herself and instead just said,

"Please do."

"You go to their school right? Jason said you met them, Tyler, Steve and Brandon?" he said.

"Sure," was all Isabella replied with.

"Maybe they can help you. They might be here by now, let's go see," Jeremy said as he turned for the stairs.

Isabella doubted the random boys who were friends with these boys could be of any help, but at least Jeremy was acting like he cared. She appreciated it. Until the boy flipped the lights off without letting her down. The steps were just wide enough to let two people use them at once. There was no railing on her left, added that it was pitch black, she was sure she would fall off.

"Stop, let me down," Isabella said in a whiny voice.

"Do you trust me?" Jeremy asked.

"No," she answered with complete honesty.

"Well, you should. You'll be fine," he said as he rubbed her left leg he was holding onto. This added more uneasiness. The girl couldn't resist and found herself trying to gain some soft of grip on the boy's head to gain balance. Grabbing his ears didn't work. She couldn't wrap around his neck without choking him. She settled on having her fingers through his short hair while both palms were clamped on either side of his skull. After a few rounds of inhaling through the nose and exhaling out of the mouth, Isabella saw the light of the hallway appear and felt a trickle of relief run through her.

Upon reaching the top of the stairs, Isabella saw Jackson walking through the hall. When he saw the two, Jackson went back to the living room where the girl could still hear him request that Mark give him a shoulder ride.

"Now will you please let me down?" Isabella asked with her hands still on his head.

"Should I?" Jeremy asked.

"Should I try to jump off?" Isabella asked. This must of let the boy know she was serious since he started to crouch down. Once she was down and on her own two feet, the girl looked him in the eye and shook her head before walking to the living room. This caused the boy to smile before letting out a small laugh.

Now in the room were the three boys she had lunch with on Monday along with the other three who looked unmoved from when she saw them last. Except for Jackson who now had his head Mark's lap and was laying on the couch. With the way too comfortable chair now occupied by the tall boy she think was named Tyler, she went and sat on the far end of the couch Jason and the boy she think was Steve sat on.

CHAPTER 18

Isabella sat as a silent member of the conversation she was drifting in and out of. All the boys were talking about things she didn't know of laced with inside jokes that had them howling. She spent most of the night watching whatever dramas Jackson had on screen from her spot between Jason and Jeremy. The night passed with her only speaking when spoken to and trying her best not to fall asleep. Once the boys started announcing their departures, Isabella payed attention. One by one the guys left, sometimes winking or making a stupid gesture towards the girl until she was left alone with Jeremy.

After the room was cleared, Isabella tried her best to be subtle while scooting away from the boy. He looked at her and pouted.

"You said you'd get my things back, right?" she asked, wishing she had her phone with her.

"I called my dad and he wouldn't be able to pick it up until Thursday," he said, leaning his body away from the armrest and towards her. She frowned but nodded at his statement nonetheless.

"So I'm spending the night?" she asked, ready to go to bed. The boy smiled and nodded.

"And we can cuddle in peace," he said, nearly holding his chin in the palms of his hands. The girl scrunched her nose at him.

"I'll be fine on the couch, by myself, thank you," she said. The boy pouted again as if it was his part time job.

"That won't be good for your back, a bed will be much better, come on," he said while grabbing her hand and standing up. The girl was a bit weary of what he had in mind. But she thought to wait until he fell asleep then sneak off and lay on one of the couches.

Jeremy took her down a different hallway than before and up a flight of stairs. This time it was lit up and so were some of the rooms on the second floor. Isabella thought of how her parents would have a fit if she left all of the lights on like this. They walked further, turned a corner, kept the pace down another corridor and turned again. Before them at the end of this hall was a single door. The girl couldn't find her way downstairs even if she wanted to. The boy opened the door and flipped on a light. Once the area was illuminated, Isabella saw that it was a pig sty. It didn't stink, which seemed magical considering the floor was covered with dirty clothes and messy dishes. Half empty water bottles lined the window sill. Centered between two tables was a massive bed, the comforter invisible due to loads of papers containing a several lines of writing on each page. A guitar laid on top of a dresser, threatening to fall off. When the boy tugged on her hand to lead her in, she stood her ground.

"Your room is filthy, I'm not sleeping in here. We can both sleep on the couch for all I care," she said, looking him straight in the eyes. He tilted his head and looked around the room as if she were seeing things. Isabella let go of his hand and turned around.

"I'll be downstairs if you need me, goodnight!" she called out from the end of the hallway. Turning right led into a dead end. She spun around and came face to face with a crossed-arm Jeremy who had his right eyebrow raised. She ignored him and tried to walk past. He stopped her and put one arm around her shoulders and the other behind her knees, forcing her to fall into him. He picked her up and carried her.

"Let's go the guest bedroom," he said while turning a corner and started down the stairs.

The next morning Isuel woke up in the bed alone. She sat up and took inventory of her surroundings until she noticed a note on the bedside table. The girl got on her feet and picked up the piece of paper. In sloppy delicate writing it told her that Jeremy left for work and would be back with his father around nine. After that he would show her something. She sat the note down and walked out of the room. Two steps down the hall led her to the living room. She found the remote and clicked the power button. According to the channel selector on screen, it was half past noon. The girl had no idea what time she fell asleep last night, but she wasn't tired anymore.

Isabella laid on the couch and stared at the ceiling. With no one to call and nothing to do for almost nine hours, she had to get creative. Maybe explore the house? Even though she was bound to get lost, it might lead her to the truth of the situation and could learn about who this Jeremy kid really was.

The day past and hours flew faster than one could count them. Isabella walked through the halls and trailed in and out of each room. She was now in the storage room, one she saved for last due to the courage one had to muster to take the terrifying path down to the bottom. It had been the most fruitful place she searched all day. She gained the fact that there were no real family photos other than Jeremy and his father. There were a good amount of the boy and his friends and even a few of the man and some other men his age. However, there didn't seem to be any images of Jeremy's mother.

Downstairs within the piles of junk, she found things even more mysterious. The most shocking was a thing that resembled a canine or wolf skull. She wasn't sure if it was real or fake, but with how sharp the teeth felt, she wouldn't doubt it's authenticity. Isabella was skimming through a photo album full of people she's never seen before when footsteps sounded from the stairs. She looked up but kept hold of the album, not caring who saw her snooping through the family's things. What else did they expect her to do? The girl stood up from her spot on the concrete floor and peeked around the mound of junk to see Jeremy at the foot of the steps. Feeling bold, she walked over to him and pointed at a random photo and asked if he knew who they were.

"I don't know. Sorry for coming back so late," he said while taking the book from her and sitting it down on top of a random pile. "but we have to hurry," he said, grabbing her hand and leading her up the stairs, not bothering to flip the lights off. The girl was a little excited to see what was going to happen but hoped he wasn't just playing around again. Once at the top of the stairs they went through the hall and into the kitchen. Standing by the table was the man Isabella saw in a lot of photographs today.

"Isabella, this is my father," Jeremy said while gesturing towards the man. The girl gave a polite smile and small bow.

"It's nice to finally meet the girl my son has told me all about. This boy said he wanted to show you his transformation tonight. Since I'm too old to got through that anymore, you'll be sticking with me, alright?" the man said.

Isabella looked at Jeremy with a puzzled expression.

"It's for your safety, trust me," he said while giving her hand a reassuring squeeze. The gesture actually gave the girl a bit of comfort. Even though she didn't know what was happening, she felt a surge of trust and decided to nod her head. He smiled at her and looked out the window behind the table. It was pitch black outside.

"It'll be starting soon," Jeremy said to his father. He looked at the girl, before he could get a word out, the back door opened. From the other end of the kitchen Jason came in.

"Everyone is outside, hurry up," the guy said before rushing back into the night.

"Let's go," Jeremy said to his father and Isabella. He led the girl outside with the man trailing behind. Out on the deck were a few wicker chairs with pillows as cushions and a wooden bench swing, all lit up by small lights along the outside edge of the floor.

"Stay here with my dad, okay? And watch us, watch us and you'll believe everything we've said," he stated before releasing her hand and giving her a hug. The girl stood still as he ran to his friends who were stripping under the moonlight. She thought back to their extravagant tale of werewolves and war. Is that what they are going to show her?

"Sit down, get comfortable. This might take a while," the father said from his chair. The girl looked at him and let out an 'okay' while taking a seat on the swing. She kept an eye on the group of boys who were down to their boxers.

"Don't look at my butt, please," Tyler said a bit shy as he took off the last article of clothing.

"Focus on Jer's butt," Jason said with a laugh.

"You can look at me if you want," Jackson said as he did a little wiggle before removing his boxers.

Jeremy told her to watch, so she did, but did her best to keep her eyes above waist level, The girl didn't suffer too long. Soon after they were stripped, cracking noises floated through the fresh cool spring air. Most of the boys fell straight the ground but none of them cried out in pain. Isabella had no idea what show they were putting on, but it seemed too intense to be fake. When hair began to trickle out of their pale skin, covering the boys in fur, her heart wanted to pause. The first howl came from the figure she once knew as Jackson. The seven figures got up from the dirt started moving around on all fours. They had fur to match to match what used to be their hair color, even Mark, being the main attraction with his bright red color. As they wandered through the grass, she caught sight of the snouts that replaced their faces.

"Cool huh," Jeremy's dad spoke up from his spot. The girl blinked and looked at the man, then back at the boys who were no longer boys.

"They really are werewolves," she said. Jeremy's father let out a sound of agreement that Isabella barely heard. She was too overwhelmed by some foreign emotion. It wasn't fear, but far from relief. It was something that felt comfortable. Something that made her click with moment and made her feel like everything was okay. This was how things were supposed to be so she didn't have to worry anymore. The girl looked at the man who gave her a warm smile. She gazed at the group who were now taking off on their own paths through the neighboring forests.

"They'll be back before the night is over. Exhausted and naked, but they'll be our boys again," the man spoke up. The girl nodded without looking at him. She kept her eyes locked on the last wolf, taking it's time strolling into the thicket of trees.

"You know he won't let you leave," the father said.

"I don't want to leave," she said.

ABOUT THE AUTHOR

A. H. Leigh

A. H. Leigh is a twenty something romance novelist whom enjoys audiobooks, phone games and Starbucks Venti Frappuccinos.

BOOKS BY THIS AUTHOR

Game Changer

"Can you please just say yes?" Jackson Warner asked.

Yasmin was curious as to why he wouldn't leave her alone. She was more curious as to why he walked up to her in the first place. The girl liked to be by herself and tried her best to avoid talking to people at school. She was known by the kids in her class as the odd mute girl, so why the boy who played sports and cheered the loudest at games he wasn't participating in wanted to go on a date was beyond her. It was probably just a joke. Funny or not, Yasmin was not having it.

But what will happen as the pair grow closer and form an unlikely friendship? Will it bloom into a sweet romance or wither into a regrettable memory?

Made in the USA
Coppell, TX
28 March 2022